JORGE LUIS BORGES

A UNIVERSAL HISTORY OF INFAMY

Translated by
Norman Thomas di Giovanni

Allen Lane

Assistance for the translation of this volume was given
by the Ingram Merrill Foundation.

The original title of this book is *Historia universal de la infamia*, Copyright ©
Emecé Editores, S.A., Buenos Aires, 1954.

First published in the United States of America by E. P. Dutton & Co. Inc., New
York, 1972 and simultaneously in Canada by Clarke, Irwin & Co. Ltd., Toronto
and Vancouver.

Published in Great Britain in 1973.

Allen Lane
A Division of Penguin Books Ltd.
21 John Street, London WCIN 2BT
ISBN 0 7139 0448 8

Printed in Great Britain by Lowe & Brydone (Printers) Ltd., Thetford, Norfolk.
Set in Bembo.

Grateful acknowledgment is made to Seymour Lawrence/Delacorte Press for permission to reprint "The Generous Enemy," Copyright © Emecé Editores, S.A.,
and Norman Thomas di Giovanni, 1968, 1972, and to Jonathan Cape Ltd., publishers
of *The Aleph and Other Stories 1933-1969*, for permission to print "Streetcorner Man,"
which appears here in a new translation.

Parts of this book have appeared in the following places:

The Antioch Review: "Of Exactitude in Science"

Esquire: "The Widow Ching, Lady Pirate"

Harper's Magazine: "Tom Castro, the Implausible Impostor"

Intellectual Digest: "The Disinterested Killer Bill Harrigan"

New York: "Monk Eastman, Purveyor of Iniquities" (under the title "Old New
York's Classic Yegg")

The New Yorker: "The Wizard Postponed," "A Theologian in Death," "The
Mirror of Ink," "The Chamber of Statues," "Tale of the Two Dreamers" (collected
under the title "Twice-told Tales")

TriQuarterly: "The Masked Dyer, Hakim of Merv"

Western Humanities Review: "Streetcorner Man"

"The Generous Enemy" first appeared in *Selected Translations 1948-1968* by W. S.
Merwin (Atheneum Publishers); the preface to the 1954 edition, in *TriQuarterly*.

I inscribe this book to S.D.: English, innumerable and an Angel. Also: I offer her that kernel of myself that I have saved, somehow—the central heart that deals not in words, traffics not with dreams and is untouched by time, by joy, by adversities.

Contents

Preface to the 1954 Edition

I should define as baroque that style which deliberately exhausts (or tries to exhaust) all its possibilities and which borders on its own parody. It was in vain that Andrew Lang, back in the eighteen-eighties, attempted a burlesque of Pope's *Odyssey*; that work was already its own parody, and the would-be parodist was unable to go beyond the original text. "Baroque" is the name of one of the forms of the syllogism; the eighteenth century applied it to certain excesses in the architecture and painting of the century before. I would say that the final stage of all styles is baroque when that style only too obviously exhibits or overdoes its own tricks. The baroque is intellectual, and Bernard Shaw has stated that all intellectual labor is essentially humorous. Such humor is not deliberate in the work of Baltasar Gracián, but is deliberate, or self-conscious, in John Donne's.

The very title of these pages flaunts their baroque character. To curb them would amount to destroying them; this is why I now prefer to invoke the pronouncement "What I have written I have written" (John 19:22) and to reprint them, twenty years later, as they stand. They are the irresponsible game of a shy young man who dared not write stories and so amused himself by falsifying and distorting (without any aesthetic justification whatever) the tales of others. From these ambiguous exercises, he went on to the labored composition of a straightforward story—"Streetcorner Man"—which he signed with the name of one of his great grandfathers, Francisco Bustos, and which has enjoyed an unusual and somewhat mystifying success.

In that story, which is about life on the outer edge of old-time Buenos Aires, it will be noted that I have introduced a few cultivated words—"intestines," "involutions," and so forth. I did so because the hoodlum aspires to refinement, or (this reason invalidates the other but is perhaps the true one) because hoodlums are individuals and do not always speak like The Hoodlum, who is a platonic type.

The theologians of the Great Vehicle point out that the essence of the universe is emptiness. Insofar as they refer to that particle of the universe which is this book, they are entirely right. Scaffolds and pirates populate it, and the word "infamy" in the title is thunderous, but behind the sound and fury there is nothing. The book is no more than appearance, than a surface of images; for that very reason, it may prove enjoyable. Its author was a somewhat unhappy man, but he amused himself writing it; may some echo of that pleasure reach the reader.

In the "Etcetera" section, I have added three new pieces.

J.L.B.

Preface to the First Edition

The exercises in narrative prose that make up this book were written in 1933 and 1934. They stem, I believe, from my re-readings of Stevenson and Chesterton, and also from Sternberg's early films, and perhaps from a certain biography of Evaristo Carriego. They overly exploit certain tricks: random enumerations, sudden shifts of continuity, and the paring down of a man's whole life to two or three scenes. (A similar concern with visual aims gives shape to the story "Streetcorner Man.") They are not, they do not try to be, psychological.

As for the examples of magic that close the volume, I have no other rights to them than those of translator and reader. Sometimes I suspect that good readers are even blacker and rarer swans than good writers. Will anyone deny that the pieces attributed by Valéry to his pluperfect Edmond Teste are, on the whole, less admirable than those of Teste's wife and friends? Reading, obviously, is an activity which comes after that of writing; it is more modest, more unobtrusive, more intellectual.

J.L.B.

Buenos Aires, May 27, 1935

A
UNIVERSAL
HISTORY
OF
INFAMY

The Dread Redeemer
Lazarus Morell

The Dread Redeemer
Lazarus Morell

The Remote Cause

In 1517, the Spanish missionary Bartolomé de las Casas, taking
great pity on the Indians who were languishing in the hellish
workpits of Antillean gold mines, suggested to Charles V,
king of Spain, a scheme for importing blacks, so that they
might languish in the hellish workpits of Antillean gold mines.
To this odd philanthropic twist we owe, all up and down the
Americas, endless things—W. C. Handy's blues; the Parisian
success of the Uruguayan lawyer and painter of Negro genre,
don Pedro Figari; the solid native prose of another Uruguayan,
don Vicente Rossi, who traced the origin of the tango to
Negroes; the mythological dimensions of Abraham Lincoln;
the five hundred thousand dead of the Civil War and its three
thousand three hundred millions spent in military pensions;
the entrance of the verb "to lynch" into the thirteenth edition
of the dictionary of the Spanish Academy; King Vidor's im-
petuous film *Hallelujah*; the lusty bayonet charge led by the
Argentine captain Miguel Soler, at the head of his famous
regiment of "Mulattoes and Blacks," in the Uruguayan battle
of Cerrito; the Negro killed by Martín Fierro; the deplorable

Cuban rumba "The Peanut Vender"; the arrested, dungeon-ridden Napoleonism of Toussaint L'Ouverture; the cross and the snake of Haitian voodoo rites and the blood of goats whose throats were slit by the *papaloi's* machete; the *habanera*, mother of the tango; another old Negro dance, of Buenos Aires and Montevideo, the *candombe*.

And, further, the great and blameworthy life of the nefarious redeemer Lazarus Morell.

The Place

The Father of Waters, the Mississippi, the largest river in the world, was the worthy theater of this peerless scoundrel. (Álvarez de Pineda discovered the river, and its earliest explorer was Captain Hernando de Soto, the old conqueror of Peru, who helped while away the Inca chief Atahualpa's months of prison, teaching him the game of chess. When de Soto died, he was given the Mississippi's waters for a grave.)

The Mississippi is a broad-bosomed river, an immense, dim brother of the Paraná, the Uruguay, the Amazon, and the Orinoco. It is a river of muddy waters; each year, disgorged by it, over four hundred million tons of silt profane the Gulf of Mexico. From time immemorial, so much muck has built up a delta, where gigantic swamp cypresses grow out of the debris of a continent in perpetual dissolution, and where labyrinths of mud and rushes and dead fish extend the bounds and the peace of this foul-smelling alluvial domain. Upstream, between the Arkansas and the Ohio, is another stretch of lowlands. Living there is a sallow race of squalid men, prone to fever, who avidly gape at stone and iron, for in their environs there is little but sand, timber, and muddy water.

The Men

At the beginning of the nineteenth century (the date that concerns us), the vast cotton plantations along the river were worked, from sunup to sundown, by blacks. These blacks slept on dirt floors in wooden cabins. Apart from mother-child relations, kinships were casual and unclear. They had first names, but they made do without family names. Nor could they read. Their soft, falsetto voices intoned an English of drawled vowels. They worked in rows, bent under the overseer's lash. When they ran away, full-bearded men, springing onto beautiful horses, tracked them down with snarling packs of hounds.

To successive layers of animal hopes and African fears there had been added the words of the Bible. Their faith, therefore, lay in Christ. They sang deeply and in chorus, "Go down, Moses." The Mississippi served them as a magnificent image of the paltry Jordan.

The owners of this hard-worked land and of these black gangs were idle, greedy gentlemen with flowing locks, who lived in big mansions that overlooked the river—always with a white pine, Greek Revival portico. A good slave was worth a thousand dollars and did not last long. Some of them were thankless enough to fall ill and die. Out of such uncertainties, one had to wring the greatest return. This is why slaves were kept in the fields from first light to last; this is why plantations required yearly crops, such as cotton or tobacco or sugarcane. The soil, overworked and mismanaged by this greedy cultivation, was left exhausted within a short time, and tangled, miry wastes encroached upon the land. On abandoned farms, on the outskirts of towns, among the thick canebrakes, and in the abject bayous lived the poor whites. They were fishermen, occasional hunters, and horse thieves. They often begged bits of stolen food from the blacks, and even in their lowly condition these poor whites kept up a certain pride—that of their untainted, unmixed blood. Lazarus Morell was one of them.

The Man

The daguerreotypes of Morell usually published in American magazines are not authentic. This lack of genuine representations of so memorable and famous a man cannot be accidental. We may suppose that Morell resisted the camera, essentially, so as not to leave behind pointless clues, and, at the same time, to foster the mystery that surrounded him. We know, however, that as a young man he was not favored with looks, and that his eyes, which were too close together, and his straight lips were not prepossessing. Thereafter, the years conferred upon him that majesty peculiar to white-haired scoundrels and daring, unpunished criminals. He was an old Southern gentleman, despite a miserable childhood and an inglorious life. Versed in Scripture, he preached with unusual conviction. "I saw Lazarus Morell in the pulpit," noted the proprietor of a Baton Rouge gambling house, "and I listened to his edifying words and I saw the tears gather in his eyes. I knew that in God's sight he was an adulterer, a Negro-stealer, and a murderer, but my eyes wept, too."

Another fair record of these holy effusions is furnished by Morell himself. "I opened my Bible at random," he wrote, "and came upon a fitting verse from Saint Paul, and I preached an hour and twenty minutes. Nor was this time misspent by my assistant Crenshaw and his confederates, for they were outside rounding up all the hearers' horses. We sold them on the Arkansas side of the river, except for one spirited chestnut that I reserved for my own private use. He pleased Crenshaw as well, but I made him see that the animal was not for him."

The Method

The stealing of horses in one state and selling them in another were barely more than a digression in Morell's criminal career, but they foreshadowed the method that now assures him his rightful place in a Universal History of Infamy. This method is unique not only for the peculiar circumstances that distinguished it but also for the sordidness it required, for its deadly manipulation of hope, and for its step by step development, so like the hideous unfolding of a nightmare. Al Capone and Bugs Moran were later to operate in a great city, with dazzling sums of money and lowly submachine guns, but their affairs were vulgar. They merely vied for a monopoly. As to numbers of men, Morell came to command some thousand—all sworn confederates. Two hundred of them made up the Heads, or Council, and they gave the orders that the remaining eight hundred carried out. All the risks fell upon these active agents, or strikers, as they were called. In the event of trouble, it was they who were handed over to justice or thrown into the Mississippi with a stone fixed securely about their feet. A good many of them were mulattoes. Their diabolical mission was the following:

Flashing rings on their fingers to inspire respect, they

traveled up and down the vast plantations of the South. They would pick out a wretched black and offer him freedom. They would tell him that if he ran away from his master and allowed them to sell him, he would receive a portion of the money paid for him, and they would then help him escape again, this second time sending him to a free state. Money and freedom, the jingle of silver dollars together with his liberty—what greater temptation could they offer him? The slave became emboldened for his first escape.

The river provided the natural route. A canoe; the hold of a steamboat; a scow; a great raft as big as the sky, with a cabin at the point or three or four wigwams—the means mattered little, what counted was feeling the movement and the safety of the unceasing river. The black would be sold on some other plantation, then run away again to the canebrakes or the morasses. There his terrible benefactors (about whom he now began to have serious misgivings) cited obscure expenses and told him they had to sell him one final time. On his return, they said, they would give him part of both sales and his freedom. The man let himself be sold, worked for a while, and on his final escape defied the hounds and the whip. He then made his way back bloodied, sweaty, desperate, and sleepy.

Final Release

The legal aspect of these doings must now be reviewed. The runaway slave was not put up for sale by Morell's gang until his first master had advertised and offered a reward to any man who would catch him. An advertisement of this kind warranted the person to take the property, if found. The black then became a property in trust, so that his subsequent sale was only a breach of trust, not stealing. Redress by a civil action for such a breach was useless, as the damages were never paid.

All this was very reassuring—but not entirely foolproof. The black, out of sheer gratitude or misery, might open his mouth. A jug of rye whiskey in some Cairo brothel, where the son of a bitch, born a slave, would squander those good dollars that they had no business letting him have, and their secret was spilled. Throughout these years, abolitionist agitators roamed the length and breadth of the North—a mob of dangerous madmen who opposed private property, preached the emancipation of slaves, and incited them to run away. Morell was not going to let himself be taken in by those anarchists. He was no Yankee, he was a Southern white, the son and grandson of whites, and he hoped one day to retire from business and become a gentleman and have his own miles of cotton fields and rows of bent-over slaves. He was not about to take pointless risks—not with his experience.

The runaway expected his freedom. Lazarus Morell's shadowy mulattoes would give out an order among themselves that was sometimes barely more than a nod of the head, and the slave would be freed from sight, hearing, touch, day, infamy, time, his benefactors, pity, the air, the hound packs, the world, hope, sweat, and himself. A bullet, a knife, or a blow, and the Mississippi turtles and catfish would receive the last evidence.

The Cataclysm

In the hands of reliable men, the business had to prosper. At the beginning of 1834, Morell had already "emancipated" some seventy blacks, and many others were ready to follow the lead of these lucky forerunners. The field of operations grew wider, and it became essential to take on new associates. Among those who swore to the oath was a young man from Arkansas, one Virgil Stewart, who very soon made himself conspicuous for his cruelty. Stewart was the nephew of a gentleman who had had many slaves decoyed away. In August, 1834, this young man broke his oath and exposed Morell and his whole gang. Morell's house in New Orleans was surrounded by the authorities. Only due to their negligence, or perhaps through a bribe, was Morell able to make good an escape.

Three days passed. During this time, Morell remained hidden on Toulouse Street in an old house with courtyards that were filled with vines and statues. It seems that he took to eating little and would stalk up and down the dim, spacious rooms in his bare feet, smoking thoughtful cigars. By a slave of the place, he sent two letters to Natchez and a third to Red River. On the fourth day, three men joined him, and they stayed until dawn, arguing over plans. On the fifth day, Morell got out of bed as it was growing dusk and, asking for a razor, carefully shaved off his beard. Then he dressed and left. At an easy pace, he made his way across the city's northern suburbs. Once in the country, skirting the Mississippi flats, he walked more briskly.

His scheme was foolhardy. He planned to enlist the services

of the last men still to owe him honor—the South's obliging blacks. They had watched their companions run off and never seen them reappear. Their freedom, therefore, was real. Morell's object was to raise the blacks against the whites, to capture and sack New Orleans, and to take possession of the territory. Morell, brought down and nearly destroyed by Stewart's betrayal, contemplated a nationwide response—a response in which criminal elements would be exalted to the point of redemption and a place in history. With this aim, he started out for Natchez, where he enjoyed greater strength. I copy his account of that journey:

I walked four days, and no opportunity offered for me to get a horse. The fifth day, about twelve, I stopped at a creek to get some water and rest a little. While I was sitting on a log, looking down the road the way that I had come, a man came in sight riding on a good-looking horse. The very moment I saw him, I was determined to have his horse. I arose and drew an elegant rifle pistol on him and ordered him to dismount. He did so, and I took his horse by the bridle and pointed down the creek, and ordered him to walk before me. He went a few hundred yards and stopped. I made him undress himself. He said, "If you are determined to kill me, let me have time to pray before I die." I told him I had no time to hear him pray. He dropped on his knees, and I shot him through the back of the head. I ripped open his belly and took out his entrails, and sunk him in the creek. I then searched his pockets, and found four hundred dollars and thirty-seven cents, and a number of papers that I did not take time to examine. His boots were brand-new, and fitted me genteelly. I put them on and sunk my old shoes in the creek.

That was how I obtained the horse I needed, and directed my course for Natchez in much better style than I had been for the last five days.

The Disruption

Morell leading rebellions of blacks who dreamed of lynching him; Morell lynched by armies of blacks he dreamed of leading—it hurts me to confess that Mississippi history took advantage of neither of these splendid opportunities. Nor, contrary to all poetic justice (or poetic symmetry), did the river of his crimes become his grave. On the second of January, 1835, Lazarus Morell died of a lung ailment in the Natchez hospital, where he had been interned under the name Silas Buckley. A fellow patient on the ward recognized him. On the second and on the fourth, the slaves of certain plantations attempted an uprising, but they were put down without a great deal of bloodshed.

Tom Castro,
the Implausible Impostor

Tom Castro,
the Implausible Impostor

Tom Castro is what I call him, for this was the name he was known by, around 1850, in the streets and houses of Talcahuano, Santiago, and Valparaiso, and it is only fitting now that he comes back to these shores—even if only as a ghost and as mere light reading—that he go by this name again. The registry of births in Wapping lists him as Arthur Orton, and enters the name under the date June 7, 1834. It is known that he was a butcher's son, that his childhood suffered the drabness and squalor of London slums, and that he felt the call of the sea. This last fact is not uncommon. Running away to sea is, for the English, the traditional break from parental authority —the road to adventure. Geography fosters it, and so does the Bible (Psalms, 107): "They that go down to the sea in ships, that do business in great waters; These see the works of the Lord, and his wonders in the deep."

Orton ran away from his familiar, dirty, brick-red streets, went down to the sea in a ship, gazed at the Southern Cross with the usual disappointment, and deserted in the Chilean port of Valparaiso. As an individual, he was at once quiet and dull. Logically, he might (and should) have starved to death, but his dim-witted good humor, his fixed smile, and his un-relieved meekness brought him under the wing of a family called Castro, whose name he came to adopt. Of this South American episode no other traces are left, but his gratefulness does not seem to have flagged, since, in 1861, he reappears in Australia still using that name—Tom Castro. There, in Sydney, he made the acquaintance of a certain Ebenezer Bogle, a Negro servant. Bogle, without being especially handsome, had about him that air of authority and assurance, that archi-tectural solidity typical of certain Negroes well along in years, in flesh, and in dignity. He had another quality, which most anthropology textbooks have denied his race—a capacity for sudden inspiration. In due time, we shall see proof of this. He was a well-mannered, upright person, whose primeval African lusts had been carefully channeled by the uses and misuses of Calvinism. Apart from receiving divine visitations (which will presently be described), Bogle was no different from other men, with nothing more distinctive about him than a longstanding, shamefaced fear that made him linger at street crossings—glancing east, west, south, and north—in utter dread of the vehicle that might one day take his life.

Orton first saw him early one evening on a deserted Sydney street corner, steeling himself against this quite unlikely death. After studying him for a long while, Orton offered the Negro his arm, and, sharing the same amazement, the two men crossed the harmless street. From that moment of a now dead and lost evening, a protectorate came into being—that of the solid, unsure Negro over the obese dimwit from Wapping. In September, 1865, Bogle read a forlorn advertisement in the local paper.

The Idolized Dead Man

Toward the end of April, 1854 (while Orton was enjoying the effusions of Chilean hospitality), the steamer *Mermaid*, sailing from Rio de Janeiro to Liverpool, went down in the waters of the Atlantic. Among those lost was Roger Charles Tichborne, an army officer brought up in France and heir of one of the leading Roman Catholic families of England. Incredible as it may seem, the death of this Frenchified young man—who spoke English with the most refined Parisian accent and awoke in others that incomparable resentment which only French intelligence, French wit, and French pedantry can touch off—was a fateful event in the life of Arthur Orton, who had never laid eyes on Tichborne. Lady Tichborne, Roger's anguished mother, refused to give credence to her son's death and had heartrending advertisements published in newspapers the world over. One of these notices fell into the soft, black hands of Ebenezer Bogle, and a masterly scheme was evolved.

The Virtues of Disparity

Tichborne was a gentleman, slight in build, with a trim, buttoned-up look, sharp features, darkish skin, straight black hair, lively eyes, and a finicky, precise way of speaking. Orton was an enormously fat, out-and-out boor, whose features could hardly be made out; he had somewhat freckled skin, wavy brown hair, heavy-lidded eyes, and his speech was dim or nonexistent. Bogle got it into his head that Orton's duty was to board the next Europe-bound steamer and to satisfy

Lady Tichborne's hopes by claiming to be her son. The plan was outrageously ingenious. Let us draw a simple parallel. If an impostor, in 1914, had undertaken to pass himself off as the German emperor, what he would immediately have faked would have been the turned-up moustache, the withered arm, the authoritarian frown, the gray cape, the illustriously be-medaled chest, and the pointed helmet. Bogle was more subtle. He would have put forward a clean-shaven kaiser, lacking in military traits, stripped of glamorous decorations, and whose left arm was in an unquestionable state of health. We can lay aside the comparison. It is on record that Bogle put forward a flabby Tichborne, with an imbecile's amiable smile, brown hair, and an invincible ignorance of French. He knew that an exact likeness of the long-lost Roger Charles Tichborne was an outright impossibility. He also knew that any resemblances, however successfully contrived, would only point up certain unavoidable disparities. Bogle therefore steered clear of all likeness. Intuition told him that the vast ineptitude of the venture would serve as ample proof that no fraud was afoot, since an impostor would hardly have overlooked such flagrant discrepancies. Nor must the all-important collaboration of time be forgotten: fourteen years of Southern Hemisphere, coupled with the hazards of chance, can wreak change in a man.

A further assurance of success lay in Lady Tichborne's un-relenting, harebrained advertisements, which showed how unshakably she believed that Roger Charles was not dead and how willing she was to recognize him.

The Meeting

Tom Castro, always ready to oblige, wrote Lady Tichborne. To confirm his identity, he cited the unimpeachable proof of two moles located close to the nipple of his left breast and that childhood episode—so painful, but at the same time so unforgettable—of his having been attacked by a nest of hornets. The letter was short and, in keeping with Tóm Castro and Bogle, was wanting in the least scruples of orthography. In the imposing seclusion of her Paris hotel, the lady read and reread the letter through tears of joy, and in a few days' time she came up with the memories her son had asked for.

On the sixteenth of January, 1867, Roger Charles Tichborne announced his presence in that same hotel. He was preceded by his respectful manservant, Ebenezer Bogle. The winter day was bright with sunshine; Lady Tichborne's weary eyes were veiled with tears. The Negro threw open wide the window blinds, the light created a mask, and the mother, recognizing her prodigal son, drew him into her eager embrace. Now that she really had him back, she could relinquish his diary and the letters he had sent her from Brazil—those cherished reflections that had nourished her through fourteen years of solitude. She handed them back with pride. Not a scrap was missing.

Bogle smiled to himself. Now he had a way to flesh out the compliant ghost of Roger Charles.

Ad Majorem Dei Gloriam

This glad reunion—which seems somehow to belong to a tradition of the classical stage—might well have crowned our

35

story, rendering certain, or at least probable, the happiness of three parties: the real mother, the spurious son, the successful plotter. Fate (such is the name we give the infinite, ceaseless chain of thousands of intertwined causes) had another end in store. Lady Tichborne died in 1870, and her relatives brought suit against Arthur Orton for false impersonation. Unburdened by solitude or tears—though not by greed—they had never believed in the obese and nearly illiterate prodigal son who appeared, straight out of the blue, from the wilds of Australia. Orton counted on the support of his numerous creditors who, anxious to be paid what was owed them, were determined that he was Tichborne.

He also counted on the friendship of the family solicitor, Edward Hopkins, and of Francis J. Baigent, an antiquary intimately acquainted with the Tichborne family history. This, however, was not enough. Bogle reasoned that, to win the game, public opinion would have to be marshaled in their favor. Assuming a top hat and rolled umbrella, he went in search of inspiration along the better streets of London. It was early evening. Bogle perambulated about until a honey-colored moon repeated itself in the rectangular basins of the public fountains. The expected visitation was paid him. Hailing a cab, he asked to be driven to Baigent's flat. Baigent sent a long letter to the *Times*, certifying that the supposed Tichborne was a shameless impostor. He signed it with the name of Father Goudron of the Society of Jesus. Other equally papist accusations soon followed. Their effect was immediate: decent people everywhere were quick to discover that Sir Roger Charles was the target of an unscrupulous Jesuitical plot.

The Hansom Cab

The trial lasted one hundred and ninety days. Something like
a hundred witnesses swore that the defendant was Tichborne
—among them, four fellow officers in the 6th Dragoon Guards.
The claimant's supporters kept on repeating that he was not
an impostor, for, had he been one, he would have made some
effort to ape his model's youthful portraits. Furthermore, Lady
Tichborne had identified him, and obviously a mother cannot
be wrong. All went well, or more or less well, until a former
sweetheart of Orton's took the stand to testify. Bogle was
unshaken by this treacherous maneuver on the part of the
"relatives"; assuming top hat and umbrella, he once again
took to the London streets in search of a visitation. We will
never know whether he found it. Shortly before reaching
Primrose Hill, there loomed out of the dark the dreaded
vehicle that had been in pursuit of him down through the
years. Bogle saw it coming, he cried out, but salvation eluded
him. Dashed violently against the stone pavement, his skull
was split by the dizzying hoofs.

The Specter

Tom Castro was the ghost of Roger Charles Tichborne, but
he was a sorry ghost animated by someone else's genius. On
hearing the news of Bogle's death, he collapsed. He went on
lying, but with failing conviction and obvious discrepancies.
It was not hard to foresee the end.

On the twenty-seventh of February, 1874, Arthur Orton,

alias Tom Castro, was sentenced to fourteen years' penal servitude. In prison, he got himself liked; this was Orton's calling. Good behavior won him a four-year reduction of sentence. When this last touch of hospitality—prison—was behind him, he toured the hamlets and centers of the United Kingdom, giving little lectures in which he alternately pleaded his innocence or his guilt. Modesty and ingratiation were so deep-seated in him that many a night he would begin by exoneration and end by confession, always disposed to the leanings of his audience.

On April 2, 1898, he died.

The Widow Ching,
Lady Pirate

The Widow Ching, Lady Pirate

Any mention of pirates of the fair sex runs the immediate risk of awakening painful memories of the neighborhood production of some faded musical comedy, with its chorus line of obvious housewives posing as pirates and hoofing it on a briny deep of unmistakable cardboard. Nonetheless, lady pirates there have been—women skilled in the handling of ships, in the captaincy of brutish crews, and in the pursuit and plunder of sea-going vessels. One such was Mary Read, who once declared that the profession of pirate was not for everyone, and that to engage in it with dignity one had, like her, to be a man of courage. At the flamboyant outset of her career, when as yet she captained no crew, one of her lovers was wronged by the ship's bully. Challenging the fellow to a duel, Mary took him on with both hands, according to the time-honored custom of the West Indies—unwieldy and none-too-sure flintlock in the left, trusty cutlass in the right. The pistol misfired, but the sword behaved as it should. . . . Along about 1720, Mary Read's daring career was cut short by a Spanish gallows at St. Jago de la Vega, in Jamaica.

Another lady buccaneer of those same seas was Anne Bonney,

a good-looking, boisterous Irishwoman, with high breasts and fiery red hair, who was always among the first to risk her neck boarding a prize. She was a shipmate and, in the end, gallowsmate of Mary Read; Anne's lover, Captain John Rackam, sported a noose on that occasion, too. Contemptuous of him, Anne came up with this harsh variant of Aisha's reproach of Boabdil: "If you had fought like a Man, you need not have been hang'd like a Dog."

A third member of this sisterhood, more venturesome and longer-lived than the others, was a lady pirate who operated in Asian waters, all the way from the Yellow Sea to the rivers of the Annam coast. I speak of the veteran widow Ching.

The Apprentice Years

Around 1797, the shareholders of the many pirate squadrons of the China seas formed a combine, to which they named as admiral a man altogether tried and true—a certain Ching. So severe was this Ching, so exemplary in his sacking of the coasts, that the terror-stricken inhabitants of eighty seaboard towns, with gifts and tears, implored imperial assistance. Their pitiful appeal did not go unheard: they were ordered to put their villages to the torch, forget their fishing chores, migrate inland, and there take up the unfamiliar science of agriculture. All this they did, so that the thwarted invaders found nothing but deserted coasts. As a result, the pirates were forced to switch to preying on ships, a form of depredation which, since it seriously hampered trade, proved even more obnoxious to the authorities than the previous one. The imperial government was quick to act, ordering the former fishermen to abandon plow and yoke and mend their nets and oars. True to their old fears, however, these fishermen rose up in revolt, and the authorities set upon another course—that of pardoning Ching by appointing him Master of the Royal Stables. Ching was about to accept the bribe. Finding this out in time, the shareholders made their righteous indignation evident in a plate of poisoned greens, cooked with rice. The morsel proving deadly, the onetime admiral and would-be Master of the Royal Stables gave up his ghost to the gods of the sea. His widow, transfigured by this twofold double-dealing, called the pirate crews together, explained to them the whole involved affair, and urged them to reject both the emperor's deceitful pardon and the unpleasant service rendered by the poison-dabbling shareholders. She proposed, instead, the plundering of ships on their own account and the election of a new admiral.

The person chosen was the widow Ching. She was a slinking woman, with sleepy eyes and a smile full of decayed teeth. Her blackish, oiled hair shone brighter than her eyes. Under her sober orders, the ships embarked upon danger and the high seas.

The Command

Thirteen years of systematic adventure ensued. Six squadrons made up the fleet, each flying a banner of a different color—red, yellow, green, black, purple, and one (the flagship's) emblazoned with a serpent. The captains were known by such names as "Bird and Stone," "Scourge of the Eastern Sea," "Jewel of the Whole Crew," "Wave with Many Fishes," and

"Sun on High." The code of rules, drawn up by the widow Ching herself, is of an unappealable severity, and its straightforward, laconic style is utterly lacking in the faded flowers of rhetoric that lend a rather absurd loftiness to the style of Chinese officialdom, of which we shall presently offer an alarming specimen or two. For now, I copy out a few articles of the widow's code:

> All goods transshipped from enemy vessels will be entered in a register and kept in a storehouse. Of this stock, the pirate will receive for himself out of ten parts, only two; the rest shall belong to the storehouse, called the general fund. Violation of this ordinance will be punishable by death.
>
> The punishment of the pirate who abandons his post without permission will be perforation of the ears in the presence of the whole fleet; repeating the same, he will suffer death.
>
> Commerce with captive women taken in the villages is prohibited on deck; permission to use violence against any woman must first be requested of the ship's purser, and then carried out only in the ship's hold. Violation of this ordinance will be punishable by death.

Information extracted from prisoners affirms that the fare of these pirates consisted chiefly of ship biscuits, rats fattened on human flesh, and boiled rice, and that, on days of battle, crew members used to mix gunpowder with their liquor. With card games and loaded dice, with the metal square and bowl of fan-tan, with the little lamp and the pipe dreams of opium, they whiled away the time. Their favorite weapons were a pair of short swords, used one in each hand. Before seizing another ship, they sprinkled their cheekbones and bodies with an infusion of garlic water, which they considered a certain charm against shot.

Each crewman traveled with his wife, but the captain sailed with a harem, which was five or six in number and which, in victory, was always replenished.

Kia-king, the Young Emperor, Speaks

Somewhere around the middle of 1809, there was made public an imperial decree, of which I transcribe the first and last parts. Its style was widely criticized. It ran:

> Men who are cursed and evil, men capable of profaning bread, men who pay no heed to the clamor of the tax collector or the orphan, men in whose undergarments are stitched the phoenix and the dragon, men who deny the great truths of printed books, men who allow their tears to run toward the North—all these are disrupting the commerce of our rivers and the age-old intimacy of our seas. In unsound, unseaworthy craft, they are tossed by storms both night and day. Nor is their object one of benevolence: they are not and never were the true friends of the seafarer. Far from lending him their aid, they swoop down on him most viciously, inviting him to wrack and ruin, inviting him to death. In such wise do they violate the natural laws of the Universe that rivers overflow their banks, vast acreages are drowned, sons are

pitted against fathers, and even the roots of rain and drought are altered. . . .

. . . In consequence, Admiral Kwo-lang, I leave to your hand the administration of punishment. Never forget that clemency is a prerogative of the throne and that it would be presumptuous of a subject to endeavor to assume such a privilege. Therefore, be merciless, be impartial, be obeyed, be victorious.

The incidental reference to unseaworthy vessels was, of course, false. Its aim was to encourage Kwo-lang's expedition. Some ninety days later, the forces of the widow Ching came face to face with those of the Middle Kingdom. Nearly a thousand ships joined battle, fighting from early morning until late evening. A mixed chorus of bells, drums, curses, gongs, and prophecies, along with the report of the great ordnance, accompanied the action. The emperor's forces were sundered. Neither the proscribed clemency nor the recommended cruelty had occasion to be exercised. Kwo-lang observed a rite that our present-day military, in defeat, choose to ignore—suicide.

The Terrorized Riverbanks

The proud widow's six hundred war junks and forty thousand victorious pirates then sailed up the mouths of the Si-kiang, and to port and starboard they multiplied fires and loathsome revels and orphans. Entire villages were burned to the ground. In one of them alone, the number of prisoners passed a thousand. A hundred and twenty women who sought the confused refuge of neighboring reedfields and paddies were betrayed by a crying baby and later sold into slavery in Macao. Although at some remove, the tears and bereavement wreaked by this depredation came to the attention of Kia-king, the Son of Heaven. Certain historians contend that this outcry pained him less than the disaster that befell his punitive expedition. The truth is that he organized a second expedition, awesome in banners, in sailors, in soldiers, in the engines of war, in provisions, in augurs, and in astrologers. The command this time fell upon one Ting-kwei. The fearful multitude of ships sailed into the delta of the Si-kiang, closing off passage to the pirate squadron. The widow fitted out for battle. She knew it would be difficult, even desperate; night after night and month after month of plundering and idleness had weakened her men. The opening of battle was delayed. Lazily, the sun rose and set upon the rippling reeds. Men and their weapons were waiting. Noons were heavy, afternoons endless.

The Dragon and the Fox

And yet, each evening, high, shiftless flocks of airy dragons rose from the ships of the imperial squadron and came gently to rest on the enemy decks and surrounding waters. They were lightweight constructions of rice paper and strips of reed, akin to comets, and their silvery or reddish sides repeated identical characters. The widow anxiously studied this regular stream of meteors and read in them the long and perplexing fable of a dragon which had always given protection to a fox, despite the fox's long ingratitude and repeated transgressions. The moon grew slender in the sky, and each evening the paper and reed figures brought the same story, with almost imperceptible variants. The widow was distressed, and she sank deep into thought. When the moon was full in the sky and in the reddish water, the story seemed to reach its end. Nobody was able to predict whether limitless pardon or limitless punishment would descend upon the fox, but the inexorable end drew near. The widow came to an understanding. She threw her two short swords into the river, kneeled in the bottom of a small boat, and ordered herself rowed to the imperial flagship.

It was dark; the sky was filled with dragons—this time, yellow ones. On climbing aboard, the widow murmured a brief sentence. "The fox seeks the dragon's wing," she said.

The Apotheosis

It is a matter of history that the fox received her pardon and devoted her lingering years to the opium trade. She also left off being the widow, assuming a name which in English means "Luster of Instruction."

> From this period [wrote one Chinese chronicler lyrically], ships began to pass and repass in tranquillity. All became quiet on the rivers and tranquil on the four seas. Men sold their weapons and bought oxen to plough their fields. They buried sacrifices, said prayers on the tops of hills, and rejoiced themselves by singing behind screens during the day-time.

Monk Eastman,
Purveyor of Iniquities

Monk Eastman,
Purveyor of Iniquities

Those of This America

Standing out sharply against a background of blue walls or open sky, two hoodlums dressed in close-fitting suits of sober black and wearing thick-heeled shoes dance a deadly dance— a ballet of matching knives—until a carnation starts from the ear of one of them as a knife finds its mark in him, and he brings the unaccompanied dance to a close on the ground with his death. Satisfied, the other adjusts his high-crowned hat and spends his final years recounting the story of this clean duel. That, in sum and substance, is the history of our old-time Argentine underworld. The history of New York's old underworld is both more dizzying and more clumsy.

Those of the Other

The history of the gangs of New York (revealed in 1928 by Herbert Asbury in a solid volume of four-hundred octavo pages) contains all of the confusion and cruelty of the barbarian cosmogonies, and much of their giant-scale ineptitude —cellars of old breweries honeycombed into Negro tenements;

a ramshackle New York of three-story structures; criminal gangs like the Swamp Angels, who rendezvoused in a labyrinth of sewers; criminal gangs like the Daybreak Boys, who recruited precocious murderers of ten and eleven; loners, like the bold and gigantic Plug Uglies, who earned the smirks of passersby with their enormous plug hats, stuffed with wool and worn pulled down over their ears as helmets, and their long shirttails, worn outside the trousers, that flapped in the Bowery breeze (but with a huge bludgeon in one hand and a pistol peeping out of a pocket); criminal gangs like the Dead Rabbits, who entered into battle under the emblem of a dead rabbit impaled on a pike; men like Dandy Johnny Dolan, famous for the oiled forelock he wore curled and plastered against his forehead, for his cane whose handle was carved in the likeness of a monkey, and for the copper device he invented and used on the thumb for gouging out an adversary's eyes; men like Kit Burns, who for twenty-five cents would decapitate a live rat with a single bite; men like Blind Danny Lyons, young and blond and with immense dead eyes, who pimped for three girls, all of whom proudly walked the streets for him; rows of houses showing red lanterns in the windows, like those run by seven sisters from a small New England village, who always turned their Christmas Eve proceeds over to charity; rat pits, where wharf rats were starved and sent against terriers; Chinese gambling dives; women like the repeatedly widowed Red Norah, the vaunted sweetheart of practically the entire Gopher gang; women like Lizzie the Dove, who donned widow's weeds when Danny Lyons was executed for murder, and who was stabbed in the throat by Gentle Maggie during an argument over whose sorrow for the departed blind man was the greater; mob uprisings like the savage week of draft riots in 1863, when a hundred buildings were burned to the ground and the city was nearly taken over; teeming street fights in which a man went down as at sea, trampled to death; a thief and horse poisoner like Yoske Nigger. All these go to weave underworld New York's chaotic history. And its most famous hero is Edward Delaney, alias William Delaney, alias Joseph Marvin, alias Joseph Morris, alias Monk Eastman— boss of twelve hundred men.

The Hero

These shifts of identity (as distressing as a masquerade, in which one is not quite certain who is who) omit his real name —presuming there is such a thing as a real name. The recorded fact is that he was born in the Williamsburg section of Brooklyn as Edward Osterman, a name later Americanized to Eastman. Oddly enough, this stormy underworld character was Jewish. He was the son of the owner of a kosher restaurant, where men wearing rabbinical beards could safely partake of the bloodless and thrice-cleansed flesh of ritually slaughtered calves. At the age of nineteen, about 1892, his father set him up in business with a bird store. A fascination for animals, an interest in their small decisions and inscrutable innocence, turned into a lifelong hobby. Years afterward, in a period of opulence, when he scornfully refused the Havana cigars of freckle-faced Tammany sachems or when he paid visits to the best houses of prostitution in that new invention, the automobile (which seemed the bastard offspring of a gondola), he started a second business, a front, that accommodated a hundred cats and more than four hundred pigeons—none of which were for sale to anyone. He loved each one, and often he strolled through his neighborhood with a happy cat under an arm, while several others trailed eagerly behind.

He was a battered, colossal man. He had a short, bull neck; a barrel chest; long, scrappy arms; a broken nose; a face, although plentifully scarred, less striking than his frame; and legs bowed like a cowboy's or a sailor's. He could usually be found without a shirt or coat, but not without a derby hat several sizes too small perched on his bullet-shaped head. Mankind has conserved his memory. Physically, the conventional moving-picture gunman is a copy of him, not of the pudgy, epicene Capone. It is said of Louis Wolheim that Hollywood employed him because his features suggested those of the lamented Monk Eastman. Eastman used to strut about his underworld kingdom with a great blue pigeon on his shoulder, just like a bull with a cowbird on its rump.

Back in the mid-nineties, public dance halls were a dime a dozen in the city of New York. Eastman was employed in one of them as a bouncer. The story is told that a dance-hall manager once refused to hire him, whereupon Monk demonstrated his capacity for the work by wiping the floor with the pair of giants who stood between him and the job. Single-handed, universally feared, he held the position until 1899. For each troublemaker he quelled, he cut a notch in his brutal bludgeon. One night, his attention drawn to a shining bald pate minding its own business over a bock beer, he laid its bearer out with a blow. "I needed one more notch to make fifty," he later explained.

The Territory

From 1899 on, Eastman was not only famous but, during elections, he was captain of an important ward. He also collected protection money from the houses of prostitution, gambling dives, streetwalkers, pickpockets, and burglars of his sordid domain. Tammany politicians hired him to stir up trouble; so did private individuals. Here are some of his prices:

Ear chawed off	$15
Leg or arm broke	19
Shot in leg	25
Stab	25
Doing the big job	100 and up

Sometimes, to keep his hand in, Eastman personally carried out a commission.

A question of boundaries (as subtle and thorny as any cramming the dockets of international law) brought Eastman into confrontation with Paul Kelly, the well-known chief of a rival gang. Bullets and rough-and-tumble fighting of the two gangs had set certain territorial limits. Eastman crossed these bounds alone one early morning and was assailed by five of Kelly's men. With his flailing, apelike arms and blackjack, Monk knocked down three of the attackers, but he was ultimately shot twice in the stomach and left for dead. Eastman closed the hot wounds with thumb and index finger and staggered to Gouverneur Hospital. There, for several weeks, life, a high fever, and death vied for him, but his lips refused to name his would-be killer. When he left the hospital, the war was on, and, until the nineteenth of August, 1903, it flowered in one shoot-out after another.

The Battle of Rivington Street

A hundred heroes, each a bit different from his photograph fading in police files; a hundred heroes reeking of tobacco smoke and alcohol; a hundred heroes wearing straw boaters with gaily colored bands; a hundred heroes afflicted, some more, some less, with shameful diseases, tooth decay, complaints of the respiratory tracts or kidneys; a hundred heroes as insignificant or splendid as those of Troy or Bull Run—these hundred let loose this black feat of arms under the shadows of the arches of the Second Avenue elevated. The cause was the attempted raid by Kelly's gunmen on a stuss game operated by a friend of Eastman's on Rivington Street. One of the gunmen was killed, and the ensuing flurry of shots swelled into a battle of uncounted revolvers. Sheltered behind the pillars of the elevated structure, smooth-shaven men quietly blazed away at each other and became the focus of an awesome ring of rented automobiles loaded with eager reinforcements, each bearing a fistful of artillery.

What did the protagonists of this battle feel? First (I believe), the brutal conviction that the senseless din of a hundred revolvers was going to cut them down at any moment; second (I believe), the no less mistaken certainty that if the first shots did not hit them they were invulnerable. What is without doubt, however, is that, under cover of the iron pillars and the night, they fought with a vengeance. Twice the police intervened, and twice they were driven off. At the first glimmer of dawn, the battle petered out—as if it were obscene or ghostly. Under the great arches of the elevated were left seven critically wounded men, four corpses, and one dead pigeon.

The Creakings

The local politicians, in whose ranks Monk Eastman served, always publicly denied that such gangs existed, or else claimed that they were mere sporting clubs. The indiscreet battle of Rivington Street now alarmed them. They arranged a meeting between Eastman and Kelly in order to suggest to them the need for a truce. Kelly (knowing very well that Tammany Hall was more effective than any number of Colts when it came to obstructing police action) agreed at once; Eastman (with the pride of his great, brutish hulk) hungered for more blasting and further frays. He began to refuse, and the politicians had to threaten him with prison. In the end, the two famous gangsters came face to face in an unsavory dive, each with a huge cigar between his teeth, a hand on his revolver, and his watchful thugs surrounding him. They arrived at a typically American decision: they would settle their dispute in the ring by squaring off with their fists. Kelly was an experienced boxer. The fight took place in a barn up in the Bronx, and it was an extravagant affair. A hundred and forty spectators looked on, among them mobsters with rakish derbies and their molls with enormous coiffures in which weapons were sometimes concealed. The pair fought for two hours and it ended in a draw. Before a week was out, the shooting started up again. Monk was arrested for the nth time. With great relief, Tammany Hall washed their hands of him; the judge prophesied for him, with complete accuracy, ten years of prison.

Eastman vs. Germany

When the still puzzled Monk was released from Sing Sing, the twelve hundred members of his gang had broken up into warring factions. Unable to reorganize them, he took to operating on his own. On the eighth of September, 1917, he was arrested for creating a disturbance in a public thoroughfare. The next day, deciding to take part in an even larger disturbance, he enlisted in the 106th Infantry of the New York National Guard. Within a few months, he was shipped overseas with his regiment.

We know about various aspects of his campaign. We know that he violently disapproved of taking prisoners and that he once (with just his rifle butt) interfered with that deplorable practice. We know that he managed to slip out of the hospital three days after he had been wounded and make his way back to the front lines. We know that he distinguished himself in the fighting around Montfaucon. We know that he later held that a number of little dance halls around the Bowery were a lot tougher than the war in Europe.

The Mysterious, Logical End

On Christmas Day, 1920, Monk Eastman's body was found at dawn on one of the downtown streets of New York. It had five bullet wounds in it. Happily unaware of death, an alley cat hovered around the corpse with a certain puzzlement.

The Disinterested Killer
Bill Harrigan

The Disinterested Killer
Bill Harrigan

An image of the desert wilds of Arizona, first and foremost,
an image of the desert wilds of Arizona and New Mexico—
a country famous for its silver and gold camps, a country of
breathtaking open spaces, a country of monumental mesas and
soft colors, a country of bleached skeletons picked clean by
buzzards. Over this whole country, another image—that of
Billy the Kid, the hard rider firm on his horse, the young man
with the relentless six-shooters, sending out invisible bullets
which (like magic) kill at a distance.

The desert veined with precious metals, arid and blinding-
bright. The near child who on dying at the age of twenty-one
owed to the justice of grown men twenty-one deaths—"not
counting Mexicans."

The Larval Stage

Along about 1859, the man who would become known to
terror and glory as Billy the Kid was born in a cellar room of
a New York City tenement. It is said that he was spawned
by a tired-out Irish womb but was brought up among Negroes.

In this tumult of lowly smells and woolly heads, he enjoyed a superiority that stemmed from having freckles and a mop of red hair. He took pride in being white; he was also scrawny, wild, and coarse. At the age of twelve, he fought in the gang of the Swamp Angels, that branch of divinities who operated among the neighborhood sewers. On nights redolent of burnt fog, they would clamber out of that foul-smelling labyrinth, trail some German sailor, do him in with a knock on the head, strip him to his underwear, and afterward sneak back to the filth of their starting place. Their leader was a gray-haired Negro, Gas House Jonas, who was also celebrated as a poisoner of horses.

Sometimes, from the upper window of a waterfront dive, a woman would dump a bucket of ashes upon the head of a prospective victim. As he gasped and choked, Swamp Angels would swarm him, rush him into a cellar, and plunder him.

Such were the apprentice years of Billy Harrigan, the future Billy the Kid. Nor did he scorn the offerings of Bowery playhouses, enjoying in particular (perhaps without an inkling that they were signs and symbols of his destiny) cowboy melodramas.

Go West!

If the jammed Bowery theaters (whose top-gallery riffraff shouted "Hoist that rag!" when the curtain failed to rise promptly on schedule) abounded in these blood and thunder productions, the simple explanation is that America was then experiencing the lure of the Far West. Beyond the sunset lay the goldfields of Nevada and California. Beyond the sunset were the redwoods, going down before the ax; the buffalo's huge Babylonian face; Brigham Young's beaver hat and plural bed; the red man's ceremonies and his rampages; the clear air of the deserts; endless-stretching range land; and the earth itself, whose nearness quickens the heart like the nearness of the sea. The West beckoned. A slow, steady rumor populated those years—that of thousands of Americans taking possession of the West. On that march, around 1872, was Bill Harrigan, treacherous as a bull rattler, in flight from a rectangular cell.

The Demolition of a Mexican

History (which, like certain film directors, proceeds by a series of abrupt images) now puts forward the image of a danger-filled saloon, located—as if on the high seas—out in the heart of the all-powerful desert. The time, a blustery night of the year 1873; the place, the Staked Plains of New Mexico. All around, the land is almost uncannily flat and bare, but the sky, with its storm-piled clouds and moon, is full of fissured cavities and mountains. There are a cow's skull, the howl and the eyes of coyotes in the shadows, trim horses, and from the saloon an elongated patch of light. Inside, leaning over the bar, a group of strapping but tired men drink a liquor that warms them for a fight; at the same time, they make a great show of large silver coins bearing a serpent and an eagle. A drunk croons to himself, poker-faced. Among the men are several who speak a language with many s's, which must be Spanish, for those who speak it are looked down on. Bill Harrigan, the red-topped tenement rat, stands among the drinkers. He has downed a couple of *aguardientes* and thinks of asking for one more, maybe because he hasn't a cent left. He is somewhat overwhelmed by these men of the desert. He sees them as imposing, boisterous, happy, and hatefully wise in the handling of wild cattle and big horses. All at once there is dead silence, ignored only by the voice of the drunk, singing out of tune. Someone has come in—a big, burly Mexican, with the face of an old Indian squaw. He is endowed with an immense sombrero and with a pair of six-guns at his side. In awkward English, he wishes a good evening to all the gringo sons of bitches who are drinking. Nobody takes up the challenge. Bill asks who he is, and they whisper to him, in fear, that the Dago—that is, the Diego—is Belisario Villagrán, from Chihuahua. At once, there is a resounding blast. Sheltered by that wall of tall men, Bill has fired at the intruder. The glass drops from Villagrán's hand; then the man himself drops. He does not need another bullet. Without deigning to glance at the showy dead man, Bill picks up his end of the conversation. "Is that so?" he drawled. "Well, I'm Billy the Kid, from New York." The drunk goes on singing, unheeded.

One may easily guess the apotheosis. Bill gives out handshakes all around and accepts praises, cheers, and whiskeys. Someone notices that there are no notches on the handle of his revolver and offers to cut one to stand for Villagrán's death. Billy the Kid keeps this someone's razor, though he says that "It's hardly worthwhile noting down Mexicans." This, perhaps, is not quite enough. That night, Bill lays out his blanket beside the corpse and—with great show—sleeps till daybreak.

Deaths for Deaths' Sake

Out of that lucky blast (at the age of fourteen), Billy the Kid the hero was born, and the furtive Bill Harrigan died. The boy of the sewer and the knock on the head rose to become a man of the frontier. He made a horseman of himself, learning to ride straight in the saddle—Wyoming- or Texas-style—and not with his body thrown back, the way they rode in Oregon and California. He never completely matched his legend, but he kept getting closer and closer to it. Something of the New York hoodlum lived on in the cowboy; he transferred to Mexicans the hate that had previously been inspired in him by Negroes, but the last words he ever spoke were (swear) words in Spanish. He learned the art of the cowpuncher's maverick life. He learned another, more difficult art—how to lead men. Both helped to make him a good cattle rustler. From time to time, Old Mexico's guitars and whorehouses pulled on him.

With the haunting lucidity of insomnia, he organized populous orgies that often lasted four days and four nights. In the end, glutted, he settled accounts with bullets. While his trigger finger was unfailing, he was the most feared man (and perhaps the most anonymous and most lonely) of that whole frontier. Pat Garrett, his friend, the sheriff who later killed him, once told him, "I've had a lot of practice with the rifle shooting buffalo."

"I've had plenty with the six-shooter," Billy replied modestly. "Shooting tin cans and men."

The details can never be recovered, but it is known that he was credited with up to twenty-one killings—"not counting Mexicans." For seven desperate years, he practiced the extravagance of utter recklessness.

The night of the twenty-fifth of July, 1880, Billy the Kid came galloping on his piebald down the main, or only, street of Fort Sumner. The heat was oppressive and the lamps had not been lighted; Sheriff Garrett, seated on a porch in a rocking chair, drew his revolver and sent a bullet through the Kid's belly. The horse kept on; the rider tumbled into the dust of the road. Garrett got off a second shot. The townspeople (knowing the wounded man was Billy the Kid) locked their window shutters tight. The agony was long and blasphemous. In the morning, the sun by then high overhead, they began drawing near, and they disarmed him. The man was gone. They could see in his face that used-up look of the dead.

He was shaved, sheathed in ready-made clothes, and displayed to awe and ridicule in the window of Fort Sumner's biggest store. Men on horseback and in buckboards gathered for miles and miles around. On the third day, they had to use make-up on him. On the fourth day, he was buried with rejoicing.

The Insulting Master
of Etiquette
Kôtsuké no Suké

The Insulting Master
of Etiquette
Kôtsuké no Suké

The infamous subject of this tale is the insulting master of
etiquette Kira Kôtsuké no Suké, the unfortunate court official
who brought on the degradation and death of the lord of the
castle of Akô and later refused to perform hara-kiri (which,
as a nobleman, was his duty) when menaced by the vengeance
he deserved. He is a man worthy of the thanks of all human-
kind, for he awakened keen loyalties and provided the neces-
sary black occasion for an immortal undertaking. A hundred
or so novels, studies, doctoral dissertations, and operas com-
memorate the deed—to say nothing of the effusions in porce-
lain, spangled lapis lazuli, and lacquer work. The story is
served even by the versatile silver screen, since "The Learned
History of the Forty-seven Retainers"—such is its name—is
the Japanese film's most frequently recurring inspiration. The
painstakingly documented renown which these burning atten-
tions confirm is something more than justified—it strikes any
person at once as just.

I follow A. B. Mitford's account, which, in leaving out
distracting intrusions of local color, is more concerned with
the glorious episode's whole narrative sweep. These missing

Oriental touches lead me to suspect that we are dealing with a version straight from the Japanese.

The Untied Ribbon

Sometime in the vanished spring of 1702, it happened that Asano Takumi no Kami, the distinguished lord of the castle of Akô, was appointed to receive and feast an imperial envoy. Twenty-three hundred years (some of them mythological) of polished manners had nervously defined the ceremonies to be observed upon the occasion. The envoy represented the Mikado, but by way of allusion or symbol—a subtlety one had to be careful neither to overdo nor to neglect. In order to prevent blunders that could easily prove fatal, a high official from the court at Yedo preceded the envoy in the capacity of master of etiquette. At a remove from the comfort of the court and condemned to a rustic holiday which must have seemed to him a form of exile, Kira Kôtsuké no Suké took no pains in the instruction of his charge. Sometimes he exaggerated his lofty tone to the point of insolence. His pupil, the lord of the castle, tried to ignore this ridicule. He did not know how to reply to it, and a strict sense of duty held him back from all violence. Nevertheless, one day the ribbon of the master's sock had come untied and he asked the lord to tie it up for him. Although burning with rage, Takumi no Kami patiently submitted. The rude master of etiquette told him that, in truth, he was unteachable and that only a boor could tie a knot so clumsily. The lord of the castle drew his dirk and aimed a blow at the master's head. Kôtsuké no Suké ran away, his forehead barely marked with a faint thread of blood.

A few days later, the deliberations of the military council were completed, and Takumi no Kami was sentenced to commit suicide. In the central courtyard of the castle of Akô, a platform covered in red felt was erected, and on it the doomed man appeared. Having been handed a golden dagger with a jeweled handle, he publicly confessed his guilt, stripped to the waist, and, disemboweling himself with the two ritual wounds, died like a samurai. Because of the red felt the more distant spectators were unable to see blood. A gray-haired, painstaking man—he was the councillor Oishi Kuranosuké, the condemned man's second—severed the head with a stroke of his sword.

The Simulator of Infamy

Takumi no Kami's castle was confiscated, his retainers were disbanded, his family was brought to ruin, and his tarnished name became the object of curses. Rumor has it that on the very night that he killed himself, forty-seven of his retainers, forming a league, met in a mountain fastness and planned to the last detail what eventually came to pass a year later. The truth is that they were forced to proceed step by step and with great caution, and some of their meetings took place not on an inaccessible mountaintop but in a chapel in a small forest— a kind of shabby pavilion of white wood, with no other adornment than a rectangular box containing a mirror. They craved vengeance, and vengeance must have seemed to them beyond reach.

Kira Kôtsuké no Suké, the hated master of etiquette, had fortified his house, and a crowd of archers and swordsmen guarded his palanquin. He could also count on his spies, who were incorruptible, scrupulous, and stealthy. They watched and spied on no one as much as they did on the presumed ringleader of the avengers, the councillor Kuranosuké. It was only by chance that he found out, but he built his scheme for vindication upon this fact.

Kuranosuké moved to Kyoto, a city unmatched in all the empire for its autumn colors. He gave himself up to gambling dens, taverns, and houses of the worst repute. In spite of graying hair, he rubbed elbows with harlots and poets, and with even sorrier sorts. Once, thrown out of some low haunt, he fell down and spent the night asleep in the street, his head wallowing in his own vomit.

It happened that a Satsuma man saw this, and he said sadly and angrily: "Is not this, by chance, Oishi Kuranosuké, who was a councillor of Asano Takumi no Kami, who assisted his lord in death, and who, not having the heart to avenge him, gives himself up to pleasure and shame? You are unworthy the name of a samurai!"

And he trod on Kuranosuké's sleeping face, and spat upon it. When the spies reported this bit of debauchery, Kôtsuké no Suké was greatly relieved.

Things did not come to rest there. The councillor sent away his wife and younger son, and he bought himself a concubine in a brothel. This famous act of infamy gladdened his enemy's heart and made him relax in watchfulness. So it was that Kôtsuké no Suké packed off half his guard.

On one of the bitterest nights of the winter of 1703, the forty-seven retainers met in a bare, windswept garden on the outskirts of Yedo, next to a bridge and a playing-card factory.

From there, they marched forth with the banners of their lord. But before launching their raid, they sent a message to their enemy's neighbors, announcing that they were neither night robbers nor ruffians but were engaged in a military action in the name of strict justice.

The Scar

Two bands attacked Kira Kôtsuké no Suké's palace. The councillor led the first, which assaulted the front gate; the second was led by his older son, who was about to turn sixteen and who died that night. All history knows the different moments of that vivid nightmare: the tricky, dangling descent into the courtyard on rope ladders; the drum signaling the attack; the rush of the defenders; the archers posted on the four sides of the roof; the arrows' swift mission to a man's vital organs; the porcelains smeared with blood; death, burning and then icy; the wantonness and turmoil of the slaughter. Nine retainers laid down their lives; the defenders were no less brave, and they refused to give ground. Shortly after midnight, however, all resistance came to an end.

Kira Kôtsuké no Suké, the despicable root of this display of loyalty, did not turn up. Every nook and cranny of the palace was searched for him, but women and children weeping were all to be seen. At this, when the retainers began to despair of ever finding him, the councillor noticed that the quilts of the master's bed were still warm. Renewing their search, they discovered a narrow window hidden under a bronze mirror. From down below in a gloomy little courtyard, a man dressed in white stared up at them. In his right hand, he held a trembling sword. When they climbed down, the man gave himself up without a struggle. His forehead still bore a scar—the old etching of Takumi no Kami's dirk.

The bloodstained band then went down on their knees before their hated adversary, and they told him they were the retainers of the lord of the castle of Akô, for whose loss and end the master of etiquette was to blame, and they entreated him to commit suicide, as a samurai was obliged to do.

Offering this honor to such a cringing spirit was pointless. Kôtsuké no Suké was a man to whom honor was inaccessible. As the day dawned, they were forced to cut his throat.

Testimony

Their vengeance now satisfied (but without anger or commotion or pity), the retainers make their way to the temple that holds their lord's remains.

In a bucket they carry Kira Kôtsuké no Suké's unbelievable head, taking turns looking after it. They cross the countryside and the province by the full light of day. Along the way, people flock to them with blessings and tears. The Prince of Sendai invites them to his table, but they decline, replying that their lord has been waiting for nearly two years. They come to his obscure tomb and lay their enemy's head before it as an offering.

The Supreme Court passes sentence. It is what the retainers expect—they are granted the privilege of committing suicide. They all do so, some with ardent serenity, and they are laid to rest at their lord's side. Men, women, and children gather to pray at the graves of these faithful men.

The Satsuma Man

Among those who come is a boy, dusty and weary, who must have traveled a long way. He prostrates himself before Oishi Kuranosuké's tombstone and says aloud: "I saw you lying drunk by the door of a brothel in Kyoto, and I did not think you were plotting to avenge your lord; I thought you to be a faithless soldier, and I spat in your face. Now I have come to offer atonement." So saying, he performed hara-kiri.

The abbot of the temple, feeling sympathy for his deed, buried him alongside the retainers.

This is the end of the story of the forty-seven loyal men—except that it has no end, for the rest of us, who are not loyal perhaps but will never wholly give up the hope of being so, will go on honoring them with words.

The Masked Dyer,
Hakim of Merv

To Angélica Ocampo

The Masked Dyer,
Hakim of Merv

If I am not mistaken, the chief sources of information concerning Mokanna, the Veiled (or, literally, Masked) Prophet of Khurasan, are only four in number: *a*) those passages from the *History of the Caliphs* culled by Baladhuri; *b*) the *Giant's Handbook*, or *Book of Precision and Revision*, by the official historian of the Abbasids, Ibn abi Tahir Taifur; *c*) the Arabic codex entitled *The Annihilation of the Rose*, wherein we find a refutation of the abominable heresies of the *Dark Rose*, or *Hidden Rose*, which was the Prophet's holy book; and *d*) some barely legible coins unearthed by the engineer Andrusov during excavations for the Trans-Caspian Railway. These coins, now on deposit in the Numismatic Collection at Tehran, preserve certain Persian distichs which abridge or emend key passages of the *Annihilation*. The original *Rose* is lost, for the manuscript found in 1899 and published all too hastily by the *Morgenländisches Archiv* has been pronounced a forgery—first by Horn, and afterward by Sir Percy Sykes.

The Prophet's fame in the West is owed to a long-winded poem by Thomas Moore, laden with all the sentimentality of an Irish patriot.

The Scarlet Dye

Along about the year 120 of the Hegira (A.D. 736), the man
Hakim, whom the people of that time and that land were later
to style the Prophet of the Veil, was born in Turkestan. His
home was the ancient city of Merv, whose gardens and vine-
yards and pastures sadly overlook the desert. Midday there,
when not dimmed by the clouds of dust that choke its inhabitants and leave a grayish film on the clusters of black grapes,
is white and dazzling.

Hakim grew up in that weary city. We know that a brother
of his father apprenticed him to the trade of dyer—that craft
of the ungodly, the counterfeiter, and the shifty, who were to
inspire him to the first imprecations of his unbridled career.
In a famous page of the *Annihilation*, he is quoted as saying:

> My face is golden but I have steeped my dyes, dipping
> uncarded wool on second nights and soaking treated wool
> on third nights, and the emperors of the islands still com-
> pete for this scarlet cloth. Thus did I sin in the days of
> my youth, tampering with the true colors of God's
> creation. The Angel told me that the ram was not the
> color of the tiger, the Satan told me that the Almighty
> wanted them to be, and that He was availing Himself of
> my skill and my dyestuffs. Now I know that the Angel
> and the Satan both strayed from the truth, and that all
> colors are abominable.

In the year 146 of the Hegira, or Flight, Hakim was seen
no more in Merv. His caldrons and dipping vats, along with
a Shirazi scimitar and a bronze mirror, were found destroyed.

The Bull

At the end of the moon of Sha'ban, in the year 158, the desert air was very clear, and from the gate of a caravan halting place on the way to Merv a group of men sat gazing at the evening sky in search of the moon of Ramadan, which marks the period of continence and fasting. They were slaves, beggars, horse dealers, camel thieves, and butchers of livestock. Huddled solemnly on the ground, they awaited the sign. They looked at the sunset, and the color of the sunset was the color of the sand.

From the other end of the shimmering desert (whose sun engenders fever, just as its moon engenders chills), they saw three approaching figures, which seemed to be of gigantic size. They were men, and the middle one had the head of a bull. When they drew near, it was plain that this man was wearing a mask and that his companions were blind.

Someone (as in the tales of the *Arabian Nights*) pressed him for the meaning of this wonder. "They are blind," the masked man said, "because they have looked upon my face."

The Leopard

It is recorded by the Abbasids' official chronicler that the man from the desert (whose voice was singularly sweet, or so it seemed in contrast to his brutish mask) told the caravan traders that they were awaiting the sign of a month of penance, but that he was the preacher of a greater sign—that of a lifetime of penance and a death of martyrdom. He told them that he was Hakim, son of Osman, and that in the year 146 of the

81

Flight a man had made his way into his house and, after purification and prayer, had cut off his head with a scimitar and taken it to heaven. Held in the right hand of the stranger (who was the angel Gabriel), his head had been before the Lord—in the highest heaven—who entrusted it with the mission of prophesying, taught it words so ancient that their mere utterance could burn men's mouths, and endowed it with a radiance that mortal eyes could not bear. Such was his justification of the mask. When all men on earth professed the new law, the Face would be revealed to them and they could worship it openly—as the angels already worshiped it. His mission proclaimed, Hakim exhorted them to a holy war—a jihad—and to their forthcoming martyrdom.

The slaves, beggars, horse dealers, camel thieves, and butchers of livestock shunned his call. One voice shouted out "Sorcerer!" and another "Impostor!"

Someone had a leopard with him—a specimen, perhaps, of that sleek, bloodthirsty breed that Persian hunters train—and it happened that the animal broke free of its bonds. Except for the masked prophet and his two acolytes, the rest of them trampled each other to escape. When they flocked back, the prophet had blinded the beast. Before its luminous dead eyes, the men worshiped Hakim and acknowledged his supernatural powers.

The Veiled Prophet

It is with scant enthusiasm that the historian of the Abbasid caliphs records the rise of the Veiled Hakim in Khurasan. That province—much disturbed by the failure and crucifixion of its most famous chieftain—embraced the teachings of the

Shining Face with fervor and desperation, and it lay down in tribute its blood and gold. (By then, Hakim had set aside his brutish effigy, replacing it with a fourfold veil of white silk embossed with precious stones. The symbolic color of the ruling dynasty, the Banu Abbas, was black; for his Protective Veil, for his banners and turbans, Hakim chose the very opposite color—white.) The campaign began well. In the *Book of Precision*, of course, the armies of the Caliph are everywhere victorious; but as the invariable result of these victories is the removal of generals or the withdrawal from impregnable fortresses, the chary reader can surmise actual truth. At the end of the moon of Rajab, in the year 161, the famed city of Nishapur opened its metal gates to the Masked One; at the beginning of 162, the city of Asterabad did the same. Hakim's military activity (like that of a more fortunate prophet) was limited to praying in a tenor voice, elevated toward the Divinity on the back of a reddish camel, in the very thick of battle. Arrows whistled all around without ever once striking him. He seemed to court danger. On the night a group of hated lepers gathered around his palace, he had them let in, kissed them, and given them silver and gold.

The petty tasks of government were delegated to six or seven devotees. Ever mindful of serenity and meditation, the Prophet kept a harem of a hundred and fourteen blind women, who did their best to satisfy the needs of his divine body.

The Abominable Mirrors

However indiscreet or threatening they may be, so long as their words are not in conflict with orthodox faith, Islam is tolerant of men who enjoy an intimacy with God. The Prophet himself, perhaps, might not have scorned this leniency, but his followers, his many victories, and the outspoken wrath of the Caliph—who was Mohammed al-Mahdi—drove him at last into heresy. This discord, though it led to his undoing, also made him set down the tenets of a personal creed, in which borrowings from old Gnostic beliefs are nonetheless detectable.

At the root of Hakim's cosmogony is a spectral god. This godhead is as majestically devoid of origin as of name or face. It is an unchanging god, but its image cast nine shadows which, condescending to creation, conceived and presided over a first heaven. Out of this first demiurgic crown there issued a second, with its own angels, powers, and thrones, and these founded a lower heaven, which was the symmetrical mirror of the first. This second conclave, in its turn, was mirrored in a third, and this in a lower one, and so on to the number 999. The lord of this lowermost heaven is he who rules us—shadow of shadows of still other shadows—and his fraction of divinity approaches zero.

The world we live in is a mistake, a clumsy parody. Mirrors and fatherhood, because they multiply and confirm the parody, are abominations. Revulsion is the cardinal virtue. Two ways (whose choice the Prophet left free) may lead us there: abstinence or the orgy, excesses of the flesh or its denial.

Hakim's personal heaven and hell were no less hopeless:

Those who deny the Word, those who deny the Veil and the Face [runs a curse from the *Hidden Rose*], are promised a wondrous Hell: for each lost soul shall hold sway over 999 empires of fire; and in each empire, over 999 mountains of fire; and in each mountain, over 999 castles of fire; and in each castle, over 999 chambers of fire; and in each chamber, over 999 beds of fire; and in each bed he will find himself everlastingly tormented by 999 shapes of fire, which will have his face and his voice.

This is confirmed in another surviving versicle:

In this life, ye suffer in a single body; in death and Retribution, in numberless numbers of bodies.

Heaven is less clearly drawn:

Its darkness is never-ending, there are fountains and pools made of stone, and the happiness of this Heaven is the happiness of leave-taking, of self-denial, and of those who know they are asleep.

The Face

In the year 163 of the Flight (and fifth year of the Shining Face), Hakim was besieged at Sanam by the Caliph's army. There was no lack of provisions or martyrs, and the arrival of a host of golden angels was imminent. It was at this point that an alarming rumor made its way through the fortress. An adulteress in the harem, as she was strangled by the eunuchs, had cried out that the ring finger of the Prophet's right hand was missing and that all his other fingers lacked nails. This rumor spread among the faithful. From the top of a terrace, in the midst of his people, Hakim was praying to the Lord for a victory or for a special sign. Two captains, their heads bowed down, slavish—as if beating into a driving rain—tore away the Veil.

At first, there was a shudder. The Apostle's promised face, the face that had been to the heavens, was indeed white—but with that whiteness peculiar to spotted leprosy. It was so bloated and unbelievable that to the mass of onlookers it seemed a mask. There were no brows; the lower lid of the right eye hung over the shriveled cheek; a heavy cluster of tubercles ate away the lips; the flattened, inhuman nose was like a lion's.

Hakim's voice attempted one final stratagem. "Your unforgivable sins do not allow you to see my splendor—" it began to say.

Paying no heed, the captains ran him through with spears.

STREETCORNER MAN

To Enrique Amorim

Streetcorner Man

Fancy your coming out and asking me, of all people, about the late Francisco Real. Yes, I knew him, even if he wasn't from around here. His stamping ground was the Northside—that whole stretch from the Guadalupe pond to the old Artillery Barracks. I never laid eyes on him above three times, and they were all on the same night, but nights like that you don't forget. It was when La Lujanera decided to come around to my place and bed down with me, and when Rosendo Juárez disappeared from the Maldonado for good. Of course, you're not the sort of person that name would mean much to. But around Villa Santa Rita, Rosendo Juárez—or, as we called him, the Slasher—had quite a reputation. He was one of don Nicolás Paredes' boys, just as Paredes was one of Morel's gang, and he was admired for the way he handled a knife. Sharp dresser, too. He always rode up to the whorehouse on a dark horse, his riding gear decked out in silver. There wasn't a man or dog around that didn't respect him—and that goes for the women as well. Everyone knew that he had at least a couple of killings to his credit. He usually wore a soft hat with a narrow brim and tall crown, and it would sit in a cocky way on his long hair, which he slicked straight back. Lady luck smiled on him, as they say, and around Villa all of us who were younger used to ape him—even as to how he spit. But then one night we got a good look at what this Rosendo was made of.

All this may seem made-up, but what took place on that particular night started when a flashy red-wheeled buggy, jamful of men, came barreling down one of those hard-packed dirt roads out between the brick kilns and the empty lots. Two men in black were making a lot of noise twanging on guitars, and the driver kept cracking his whip at the stray dogs that snapped at the horse's legs. Sitting quiet, directly in the middle, was a man wrapped in a poncho. This was the famous Butcher—he had picked up the name working in the stockyards—and it seemed he was out for a fight and maybe even a killing.

The night was cool and welcome. Two or three of the men sat on the folded hood as though they were parading along some downtown avenue in Carnival. Much more happened that night, but it was only later that we learned about these first doings. Our gang was there at Julia's fairly early. Her dance hall, between the Gauna road and the river, was really a big shed built of corrugated sheet iron. You could spot the place from several blocks off by the noise or by the red lamp hanging out front. Julia was a darky, but she was careful to see that things ran well. There were always plenty of musicians and good booze, not to mention dancing partners who were ready to go all night. But La Lujanera, who was Rosendo's woman, had the rest beat by a mile. She's dead now, and I can tell you that years go by when I don't give her a thought anymore, but you should have seen her in her day—what eyes! One look at her could cause a man to lose sleep.

The rum, the music, the women, Rosendo talking tough and slapping each of us on the back, which to me was a sign of real friendship—well, I was as happy as could be. I had a good partner, too, who was having an easy time following my steps. The tango took hold of us, driving us along, splitting us up, then bringing us together again. All at once, in the middle of this, I seemed to feel the music growing louder. It turned out that the two guitar players riding in the buggy were coming closer and closer, and their music was mixing with ours. Then the breeze shifted, you couldn't hear them anymore, and my thoughts went back to myself and my partner and to the involutions of the dance. A half hour or so later there were blows at the door, and a big voice called out. Since it might have been the police, everything went silent. The next thing we knew, somebody began shouldering the door, and a moment later a man burst in. Oddly enough, he looked exactly like his voice.

To us he wasn't Francisco Real—not yet—but just a big lout. He was in black from head to toe, except for a reddish-brown scarf he wore draped over one shoulder. I remember his face, which had something Indian and bony about it.

The door had come flying in, striking me. Before I knew what I was doing, I was on top of the intruder, leading with a left while my right hand fished inside my vest for my knife. But I never got a chance. Steadying himself, Real put out an arm and brushed me aside. There I was, down on the floor—behind him now—my hand still inside the jacket groping for the knife. And there he was, wading forward as though nothing had happened. Just wading forward, a whole head taller than any of us, and acting as though we didn't exist. Our boys —that pack of gaping wops—backed out of his way. But only the first of them. Next in line, the Redhead was waiting, and before the newcomer could lay a hand on his shoulder, Red's knife was out and the flat of the blade was slapping Real across the face. When the others saw that, they jumped him. The hall was long, maybe more than nine or ten yards, and they drove the Butcher from one end almost to the other, roughing him up, hooting, and spitting all over him. First they hit him with their fists, then, seeing that he didn't bother to ward off the blows, they began slapping him openhanded and flicking the fringes of their scarves at him. Of course, they were also saving him for Rosendo, who stood this whole time with his back against the far wall, neither moving a muscle nor uttering a word. All Rosendo did was puff on his cigarette, a little troubled-looking and maybe already aware of what came clear to the rest of us only later on. The Butcher stayed on his feet, but blood showed on him in one or two places. The whole hooting pack was behind him now, driving him closer and closer to Rosendo. Only when the two of them came together did Real speak. He glared at Rosendo and, wiping his face on his sleeve, said something like this:

"I'm Francisco Real and I come from the Northside. I let these fools lay their hands on me because what I'm looking for is a man. Word is going around that there's someone out here in mudville who's good with a knife. They call him the Slasher. He's supposed to be tough, and I'd sure like to meet him. Maybe a nobody like me could learn something from him."

He had his say looking straight at Rosendo, and suddenly a long knife, which he must have had up his sleeve, flashed in his hand. Now, instead of pressing in, everyone opened up space for a fight—at the same time, staring at the two of them in dead silence. Even the thick lips of the blind nigger playing the fiddle were turned their way.

It was then that I heard a commotion behind me, and in the frame of the door I caught a glimpse of six or seven men who must have been part of the Butcher's gang. The oldest, a leathery-faced man with a big gray moustache and a country look about him, came in a few steps and, awed by the women and the lights, took off his hat in respect. The rest of them kept their eyes peeled, on the lookout for anything underhanded.

What was the matter with Rosendo, not moving to throw the loudmouth out? He was still quiet, still kept his eyes down. I don't know if he spit out his cigarette or whether it fell from his lips. He finally managed a few words, but they were so low that those of us at the other end of the dance floor didn't hear what he said. Francisco Real challenged him again, and again Rosendo refused to budge. At this point, the youngest of the newcomers let out a whistle. La Lujanera gave him a look that cut right through him and, with her hair swinging loose over her shoulders, she wedged through the crowd. Reaching her man, she slipped his knife out and handed it to him.

"Rosendo," she said, "I think you're going to need this."

Up under the roof was a long window that opened out over the river. Rosendo took the blade in both hands and turned it over as though he'd never seen it before. Then, raising his arms up over his head, he suddenly flipped the knife behind him—out the window and into the Maldonado. I felt a chill go through me.

"The only reason I don't carve you up is because you sicken me," the Butcher said to Rosendo, threatening to strike him. That same moment, La Lujanera threw her arms around the Butcher's neck, fixed those eyes of hers on him, and said in a fury, "Let him alone—making us think he was a man."

For a minute or so, Francisco Real was bewildered. Then, wrapping his arms around La Lujanera, he called to the musicians to play loud and strong, and he ordered the rest of us to dance. From one end of the hall to the other, the music ran like wildfire. Real danced stiffly, but he held his partner close, and in no time he had her under his spell. When they drew near the door, he shouted, "Make way, boys, she's all mine now!" And out they went, cheek to cheek, as though floating off on the tango.

I must have colored with shame. I took a turn or so with some woman or other, then dropped her. I said it was because of the heat and the crowd, and I edged around the room.

It was a nice night out, but nice for whom? The buggy stood at the alley corner. Inside it, the pair of guitars sat straight up on the seat like men—which was as much as to say that we weren't good enough even for walking off with a cheap guitar. That thought, that we were nobodies, really burned me. I snatched the carnation from behind my ear, threw it into a puddle, and stared at it a long time trying to take my mind off things. How I wished it were another day and that that night were over! The next thing I knew—it came to me almost as a relief—an elbow was shoving me aside. It was Rosendo, skulking off alone.

"You're always in the way, kid," he snarled. Maybe he was getting something off his chest; I couldn't tell. He disappeared into the dark down toward the Maldonado. That was the last I ever saw of him.

I remained there looking at the things I'd seen all my life—the wide sky, the river flowing on blindly, a horse half asleep, the dirt roads, the kilns—and I began to realize that, in the middle of the ragweed and the dump heaps and that whole forsaken neighborhood, I had sprouted up no more than a weed myself. With our big mouths and no guts, what else would grow there but trash like us? Then I thought no, that the worse the place the tougher it had to be.

At the dance hall the music was still going strong, and on the breeze came a smell of honeysuckle. It was a nice night, all right, with so many stars—some on top of others—that looking at them made you dizzy. I tried to convince myself that what had happened meant nothing to me. Still, I couldn't get over Rosendo's cowardice and the newcomer's sheer bravery. Real had even managed to get hold of a woman for the night—for that night, for the next night, and maybe forever. God knows which way the two had headed; they couldn't have wandered far. By then they were probably going at it in some ditch.

When I got back, the dance was in full swing. I slipped quietly into the crowd, noticing that a few of our boys had left and that some of the Northsiders were dancing along with everyone else. But there was no pushing or shoving. The music sounded sleepy, and the girls tangoing with the outsiders appeared to have little to say.

I was on the lookout, but not for what happened. From

outdoors, sounds came to us of a woman crying, followed by that voice that we all knew by then—but now it was low, somehow too low.

"Go on in," it told her.

There was more wailing.

"Open the door, you hear?" Now the voice sounded desperate. "Open it, you bitch—open it."

The battered door swung open and in came La Lujanera, alone and almost as though she were being herded.

"There must be a ghost out there," said the Redhead.

"A dead man, friend." It was the Butcher staggering in, his face looking like a drunk's. In the space we opened for him he took a couple of blind, reeling steps, then all at once he fell like a log. One of his friends rolled him over and propped up his head with his scarf, but that only got him smeared with blood. We could see a great gash in Real's chest. The blood was welling up and blackening the bright red neckerchief he wore under his scarf. One of the women brought rum and some scorched rags.

He was in no condition to explain. La Lujanera stared at him in a daze, her arms dangling by her sides. There was a single question on every face, and finally she got out the answer. She said that after leaving the hall they had gone to a little field and at that point a man appeared out of nowhere, challenged the Butcher to fight, and stabbed him. She swore she didn't know who the man was, but she said that he wasn't Rosendo. I wondered whether anyone would believe her.

The man at our feet was dying. It looked to me as though whoever had done the job had done it well. But the man hung on. When he knocked that second time, Julia had been brewing maté. The cup went clear around the circle and back to me before he breathed his last. As the end came, he said in a low voice, "Cover my face." All he had left was his pride; he didn't want us watching while his face went through its agony. Someone laid his hat over him, and that's how he died—not uttering a sound—under that high black crown. It was only when his chest stopped heaving that they dared uncover him. He had that exhausted look of the dead. In his day, from the Artillery Barracks all the way to the Southside, he'd been one of the bravest men around. As soon as I knew he was dead and couldn't talk, I stopped hating him.

"All dying takes is being alive," one of the girls in the crowd said. And another said, "A man's so full of pride, and now look—all he's good for is gathering flies."

The Northside gang began talking among themselves in low voices. Then two of them spoke out together, saying, "The woman killed him." After that, one of them loudly flung the accusation in her face, and the rest swarmed around her. Forgetting I had to be careful, I leaped in. What kept me from reaching for my knife I don't know. Almost everyone was gaping at me, and I said, putting them down, "Look at this woman's hands. Where would she get the strength or the nerve to knife a man?"

Then, coolly, I added, "Whoever would have dreamed that the deceased, who'd made a big name for himself in his own backyard, would end up like this? Especially out here where nothing ever happens?"

Nobody offered his hide for a whipping.

At that moment, in the dead silence, came the sound of approaching riders. It was the police. Everyone—some more, some less—had his own good reason for staying clear of the law. The best thing was to dump the body into the Maldonado. You remember the long window the knife had flown out of? Well, that's where the man in black went. Several of them lifted him up. Hands stripped him of every cent and trinket he had, and somebody even hacked off one of his fingers to steal his ring. They were very daring with a helpless corpse once a better man had laid him out. One good heave and the current did the rest. To keep him from floating, they may have cut out his intestines. I don't know—I didn't want to look. The old-timer with the gray moustache wouldn't take his eyes off me. Making the best of the commotion, La Lujanera slipped away.

When the police came in for a look around, the dance was going again. That blind fiddler could scrape some lively numbers on that violin of his—the kind of thing you never hear anymore. It was growing light outside. The fence posts on a nearby slope seemed to stand alone, the strands of wire still invisible in the early dawn.

Easy as can be, I walked the two or three blocks back to my own place. A candle was burning in the window, then all at once it went out. Let me tell you, I hurried when I saw that. Then, Borges, I put my hand inside my vest—here by the left armpit, where I always carry it—and took my knife out again. I turned the blade over, slowly. It was as good as new, innocent-looking, and there wasn't the slightest trace of blood on it.

ETCETERA

To Néstor Ibarra

A Theologian in Death

A Theologian in Death

The angels told me that when Melancthon died he was provided with a house deceptively like the one in which he lived
in this world. (This happens to most newcomers in eternity
upon their first arrival—it is why they are ignorant of their
death, and think they are still in the natural world.) All the
things in his room were similar to those he had had before—
the table, the desk with its drawers, the shelves of books. As
soon as Melancthon awoke in this new abode, he sat at his
table, took up his literary work, and spent several days writing
—as usual—on justification by faith alone, without so much
as a single word on charity. This omission being remarked by
the angels, they sent messengers to question him. "I have
proved beyond refutation," Melancthon replied to them, "that
there is nothing in charity essential to the soul, and that to
gain salvation faith is enough." He spoke with great assurance,
unsuspecting that he was dead and that his lot lay outside
Heaven. When the angels heard him say these things, they
departed.

After a few weeks, the furnishings in his room began to
fade away and disappear, until at last there was nothing left

but the armchair, the table, the paper, and his inkstand. What is more, the walls of the room became encrusted with lime, and the floor with a yellow glaze. Melancthon's own clothes were now much coarser. He wondered at these changes, but he went on writing about faith while denying charity, and was so persistent in this exclusion that he was suddenly transported underground to a kind of workhouse, where there were other theologians like him. Locked up for a few days, Melancthon fell to doubting his doctrine, and was allowed to return to his former room. He was now clad in a hairy skin, but he tried hard to convince himself that what had just happened to him was no more than a hallucination, and he went back to extolling faith and belittling charity.

One evening, Melancthon felt cold. He began examining the house, and soon discovered that the other rooms no longer matched those of his old house in the natural world. One was cluttered with instruments whose use he did not understand; another had shrunk so small that entrance was impossible; a third had not changed, but its doors and windows opened onto vast sandbanks. One of the rooms at the back of the house was full of people who worshiped him and who kept telling him that no theologian was ever as wise as he. These praises pleased him, but since some of the visitors were faceless and others seemed dead he ended up hating and distrusting them. It was at this point that he decided to write something concerning charity. The only difficulty was that what he wrote one day he could not see the next. This was because the pages had been written without conviction.

Melancthon received many visits from persons newly dead, but he felt shame at being found in so run-down a lodging.

In order to have them believe he was in Heaven, he hired a neighboring magician, who tricked the company with appearances of peace and splendor. The moment his visitors had gone—and sometimes a little before—these adornments vanished, leaving the former plaster and draftiness.

The last I heard of Melancthon was that the magician and one of the faceless men had taken him away into the sand hills, where he is now a kind of servant of demons.

From the *Arcana Cælestia* (1749–1756)
by Emanuel Swedenborg

The Chamber of Statues

The Chamber of Statues

This tale, taken from an Arab source, is of uncertain author-
ship. From internal evidence, we may infer that the writer
was a Spanish Muslim:

In ages long gone, in the kingdom of the Andalusians, there
was a city, whose name was Lebtit or Ceuta or Jaén, where
the kings had their dwelling place. In this city stood a strong
castle with leafed gates meant neither for going in nor for
coming out but only to be kept locked. Whenever a king died
and another king took the high throne after him, he set with
his own hands a new lock to the gates, until these locks num-
bered twenty-four—one for each of the kings.

After this time, it befell the kingdom that an evil man, who
was not of the royal house, usurped the throne and rather than
add a new lock, had a mind to open the twenty-four old locks
so that he might see what lay within the castle. The vizier and
the emirs beseeched him not to do this, and they hid the
iron key ring from him and told him it was easier to add one
lock than to force twenty-four. But the king persisted with
wondrous craft, saying, "I want to look upon the contents of
this castle." They then offered him all the wealth their hands

could gather—in flocks, in Christian idols, in silver and gold. Still he would not be denied, and, with his own right hand (may it burn forever!), he prized off the locks.

Inside the castle, they found figures of Arabs—in metalwork and in wood—mounted on their swift camels and horses, with turbans hanging down over their shoulders and scimitars dangling from their belts and bearing long lances in their hands. All these figures were sculptured, and they threw shadows over the floor. The forelegs of the horses, as if they were rearing up, did not touch the ground, and yet the mighty steeds did not topple or fall. Great fear was implanted in the king by these skillful figures, the more so for their discipline and perfect silence, since they all faced the same way—which was toward the west—and not a word or a trumpet blast could be heard from them. This was in the first chamber. In the second, they found the table set for Solomon, son of David —peace be on them both! It was carved from a single emerald, whose color, as everyone knows, is green, and whose hidden virtues are real yet indescribable, for they quiet tempests, protect the chastity of the owner, dispel dysentery and evil spirits, assure a favorable outcome in litigations, and bring great relief in childbearing.

In the third chamber, two books were found. One was black, and it set forth the properties of metals, the use of talismans, and the planetary laws of the days, as well as the preparation of poisons and antidotes. The other book was white, and although its letters were quite clear, no one could decipher its teaching. In the fourth chamber, they found a map of the world, figuring all its kingdoms and cities and seas and castles and perils—each one with its true name and exact shape.

In the fifth chamber, they came upon a circular mirror, made for Solomon, son of David—peace be on the twain!— whose worth was priceless, for it was of mixed metals, and he who looked into it could see the face of his fathers and his sons from the first Adam down to those who shall hear the Trumpet. The sixth chamber was filled with an elixir, a single dram of which was enough to turn three thousand ounces of silver into three thousand ounces of fine gold. The seventh chamber appeared to be empty. It was so long that even the most skilled of archers could not have shot an arrow from the entrance and hit the opposite wall. On that wall, they found carved a dire inscription. The king read it and understood it, and its words were these: "If any hand dare open the door of this castle, living warriors after the likeness of the figures here depicted will conquer the kingdom."

These things came to pass in the year 89 of the Hegira. Before this twelve-month was out, Tariq ibn-Ziyad over-powered the fortress, defeated the king, sold his women and children into slavery, and laid waste the land. So it was that the Arabs spread over the kingdom of Andalusia, with its fig trees and watered meadows in which no thirst is suffered. As to the treasures, it is widely known that Tariq, son of Ziyad, sent them to his lord the caliph, who hoarded them in the heart of a pyramid.

From the *Thousand and One Nights*, Nos. 271 & 272

Tale of the Two Dreamers

Tale of the Two Dreamers

The Arabic historian al-Ishaqi tells this story in the reign of the caliph al-Ma'mun (A.D. 786–833):

Men worthy of trust have recorded (but Allah alone is All-Knowing and All-Powerful and All-Merciful and does not sleep) that there once lived in Cairo a man who possessed great wealth, but so freehanded and liberal was he that he lost all he had, save his father's house, and in time was forced to earn his living by his own hands. He worked so hard that one night sleep overcame him at the foot of a fig tree in his garden, and in a dream he was visited by a man, drenched through and through, who took a gold coin out of his mouth and said to him, "Your fortune lies in Persia, in Isfahan; go thither and seek it."

Early the next morning, the man awoke and set out on the long journey, facing the dangers of desert wastes, of ships, of pirates, of idolaters, of rivers, of wild beasts, and of men. At last, he found his way to Isfahan, but within the gates of that city night overtook him, and he lay down to sleep in the courtyard of a mosque. Close by the mosque there was a house, and, by decree of Allah Almighty, a band of robbers entered the mosque and made its way thence to the adjoining house. But the owners of the house, aroused by the noise of the thieves, awoke and cried out for help. The neighbors, too, shouted for help, until the captain of the police arrived with his officers, and the robbers fled over the rooftops. The captain ordered a search of the mosque, and, finding there the man from Cairo, dealt him such a whipping with bamboo lashes that he was well-nigh dead.

Two days later, he came to his senses in jail. The captain sent for him and asked, "Who are you, and where are you from?"

The man said, "I am from the famed city of Cairo, and my name is Mohammed al-Maghribi." The captain asked him, "And what brought you to Isfahan?" The man chose the truth, and he said to the captain, "I was ordered by one in a dream to go to Isfahan, for my fortune awaited me there. But when I came to Isfahan, the fortune he promised me proved to be the lashing that you so generously dealt me."

Hearing this, the captain laughed until he showed his wisdom teeth, and at last he said, "O man of little wit, thrice have I dreamed of a house in Cairo in whose yard is a garden, at the lower end of which is a sundial and beyond the sundial a fig tree and beyond the fig tree a fountain and beneath the fountain a great sum of money. Yet I have not paid the least heed to this lie; but you, offspring of a mule and a devil, have journeyed from place to place on the faith of a dream. Don't show your face again in Isfahan. Take these coins and leave."

The man took the money and set out upon his homeward march. Beneath the fountain in his garden (which was the one in the captain's dream), he dug up a great treasure. And thus Allah brought abundant blessing upon him and rewarded him and exalted him. Allah is the Beneficent, the Unseen.

From the *Thousand and One Nights*, No. 351

The Wizard Postponed

The Wizard Postponed

In the city of Santiago, there was a dean who had a burning desire to learn the art of magic. Hearing that don Illán of Toledo knew more about magic than anyone else, the dean went to Toledo in search of him.

The very morning he arrived, he went straight to don Illán's and found him reading in a room at the back of his house. Don Illán received the dean cordially, and asked him to postpone telling him the object of his visit until after they had eaten. Showing his guest into pleasant quarters, don Illán said he felt very happy about the dean's visit. After their meal, the dean told don Illán why he had come, and he begged to be taught the craft of magic. Don Illán said that he already knew that his guest was a dean, a man of good standing and of good prospects, but that were he to teach him all his knowledge, the day might come when the dean would fail to repay his services—as men in high places are often wont to do. The dean swore that he would never forget don Illán's bounty and that he would always be at his call. Once they came to an agreement, don Illán explained that the magic arts could not be learned save in a place of deep seclusion, and, taking the dean by the hand, he led him to the next room, in whose floor there was a large iron ring. Before this, however, he told the serving maid to prepare partridges for supper but not to put them on to roast until he so ordered.

Don Illán and his guest lifted the ring and went down a well-worn, winding stairway until it seemed to the dean they had gone down so far that the bed of the Tagus must now be above them. At the foot of the staircase was a cell, and in it were a library of books and a kind of cabinet with magic instruments. They were leafing through the books, when suddenly two men appeared bearing a letter for the dean, written by the bishop, his uncle, in which the bishop informed him that he was gravely ill, and that if the dean wanted to find him alive he should not tarry. The news was very upsetting to the dean—for one thing, because of his uncle's illness; for another, because he would be forced to interrupt his studies. In the end, choosing to stay, he wrote an apology and sent it to the bishop.

Three days passed, and there arrived several men in mourning bearing further letters for the dean, in which he read that the bishop had died, that a successor was being chosen, and that they hoped by the grace of God that the dean would be elected. The letters advised him to remain where he was, it seeming better that he be absent during his election.

Ten days elapsed, and two finely dressed squires came, throwing themselves down at the dean's feet and kissing his hands and greeting him as bishop. When don Illán saw these things, he turned to the new prelate with great joy and said that he thanked the Lord that such good news should have come to his house. He then asked for the now vacant deanery for his son. The bishop answered that he had already set aside the deanery for his own brother but that he would find the son some post in the Church, and he begged that they all three leave together for Santiago.

They made their way to the city of Santiago, where they were received with honors. Six months passed, and messengers from the pope came to the bishop, offering him the arch-bishopric of Toulouse and leaving in his hands the naming of a successor. When don Illán heard this, he reminded the arch-bishop of his old promise and asked for the vacated title for his son. The archbishop told him that he had already set aside the bishopric for his own uncle, his father's brother, but that as he had given his word to shed favor on don Illán, they should, together with the son, all leave for Toulouse. Don Illán had no recourse but to agree.

The three set out for Toulouse, where they were received with honors and Masses. Two years passed, and messengers from the pope came to the archbishop, elevating him to the cardinalate and leaving in his hands the naming of a successor. When don Illán learned this, he reminded the cardinal of his old promise and asked for the vacant title for his son. The cardinal told him that he had already set aside the archbishopric for his own uncle, his mother's brother—a good old man— but that if don Illán and his son were to accompany him to Rome, surely some favorable opportunity would present itself. Don Illán protested, but in the end he was forced to agree.

The three then set out for Rome, where they were received with honors, Masses, and processions. Four years elapsed, and the pope died, and our cardinal was elected to the papacy by all the other cardinals. Learning of this, don Illán kissed His

Holiness's feet, reminded him of his old promise, and asked for the vacant cardinal's office for his son. The pope told don Illán that by now he was weary of his continued requests and that if he persisted in importuning him he would clap him in jail, since he knew full well that don Illán was no more than a wizard and that in Toledo he had been a teacher of the arts of magic.

Poor don Illán could only answer that he was going back to Spain, and he asked the pope for something to eat during the long sea journey. Once more the pope refused him, whereupon don Illán (whose face had changed in a strange fashion) said in an unwavering voice, "In that case, I shall have to eat the partridges that I ordered for tonight."

The serving maid came forward, and don Illán ordered the partridges roasted. Immediately, the pope found himself in the underground cell in Toledo, no more than dean of Santiago, and so taken aback with shame that he did not know what to say. Don Illán said that this test was sufficient, refused the dean his share of the partridges, and saw him to the door, where, taking leave of him with great courtesy, he wished him a safe journey home.

From the *Libro de los enxiemplos
del Conde Lucanor et de Patronio* (1335)
by Juan Manuel

The Mirror of Ink

The Mirror of Ink

All history knows that the cruelest of the rulers of the Sudan was Yaqub the Ailing, who delivered his country to the rapacity of Egyptian tax collectors and died in a palace chamber on the fourteenth day of the moon of Barmahat, in the year 1842. There are those who hold that the wizard Abd-er-Rahman al-Masmudi (whose name may be translated as the "Servant of the All-Merciful") slew him by means of a dagger or poison. That he died a natural death is more likely, however, since he was called the Ailing. Captain Richard F. Burton spoke to the wizard in 1853, and recounts the tale I quote here:

It is true that as a consequence of the conspiracy woven by my brother Ibrahim, with the treacherous and useless support of the black chiefs of Kordofan, who betrayed him, I suffered captivity in the castle of Yaqub the Ailing. My brother perished by the sword, on the blood-red skin of Justice, but I flung myself at the hated feet of the Ailing, telling him that I was a wizard, and that if he spared my life I would show him shapes and appearances still more wonderful than those of the magic lantern. The tyrant demanded an immediate proof. I asked for a reed pen, a pair of scissors, a large leaf of Venetian paper, an inkhorn, a chafing dish with some live coals in it, some coriander seeds, and an ounce of benzoin. I cut up the paper into six strips, wrote charms and invocations on the first five, and on the remaining one wrote the following words, taken from the glorious Koran: "And we have removed from thee thy veil; and thy sight today is piercing." Then I drew a magic square in the palm of Yaqub's right hand, told him to make a hollow of it, and into the center I poured a pool of ink. I asked him if he saw himself clearly reflected in it, and he answered that he did. I told him not to raise his head. I dropped the benzoin and coriander seeds into the chafing dish, and I burned the invocations upon the glowing coals. I next asked him to name the image he desired to see. He thought a moment and said, "A wild horse, the finest of those that graze along the borders of the desert." Looking, he saw a quiet, green pasture, and a minute later a horse drawing near, lithe as a leopard, with a white spot on its face. He asked me for a drove of horses as handsome as the first one, and on the horizon he saw a cloud of dust, and then the drove. It was at this point that I knew my life was spared.

From that day on, with the first streak of light in the eastern sky, two soldiers would enter my cell and lead me to the Ailing's bedchamber, where the incense, the chafing dish, and the ink were already laid out. So it was that he demanded of me, and I showed him, all the visible things of this world. This man, whom I still hate, had in his palm everything seen by men now dead and everything seen by the living: the cities, the climates, the kingdoms into which the earth is divided; the treasures hidden in its bowels; the ships that ply its seas; the many instruments of war, of music, of surgery; fair

126

women; the fixed stars and the planets; the colors used by the ungodly to paint their odious pictures; minerals and plants, with the secrets and properties they hold locked up in them; the silvery angels, whose only food is the praise and worship of the Lord; the awarding of prizes in schools; the idols of birds and kings buried in the heart of the pyramids; the shadow cast by the bull that holds up the world and by the fish that lies under the bull; the sandy wastes of Allah the All-Merciful. He saw things impossible to tell, like gaslit streets and the whale that dies on hearing the cry of a man. Once, he ordered me to show him the city called Europe. I let him see its main thorough-fare, and it was there, I believe, in that great stream of men— all wearing black and many using spectacles—that he first set eyes on the Man with the Mask.

This figure, at times in Sudanese garments and at times in uniform, but always with a veil over his face, from then on haunted the things we saw. He was never absent, and we dared not divine who he was. The images in the mirror of ink, at first fleeting or fixed, were more intricate now; they obeyed my commands without delay, and the tyrant saw them quite plainly. Of course, the growing cruelty of the scenes left us both in a state of exhaustion. We witnessed nothing but punishments, garrotings, mutilations—the pleasures of the executioner and of the merciless.

In this way, we came to the dawn of the fourteenth day of the moon of Barmahat. The circle of ink had been poured into the tyrant's hand, the benzoin and coriander cast into the chafing dish, the invocations burned. The two of us were alone. The Ailing ordered me to show him a punishment both lawful and unappealable, for that day his heart hungered to view an execution. I let him see the soldiers with their drums, the spread calfskin, the persons lucky enough to be onlookers, the executioner wielding the sword of Justice. Marveling at the sight of him, Yaqub told me, "That's Abu Kir, he who dealt justice to your brother Ibrahim, he who will seal your fate when it's given me to know the science of bringing together these images without your aid."

He asked me to have the doomed man brought forward. When this was done, seeing that the man to be executed was the mysterious man of the veil, the tyrant paled. I was ordered to have the veil removed before justice was carried out. At this, I threw myself at his feet, beseeching, "O king of time and sum and substance of the age, this figure is not like any of the others, for we do not know his name or the name of his fathers or the name of the city where he was born. I dare not tamper with the image, for fear of incurring a sin for which I shall be held to account."

The Ailing laughed, and when he finished he swore that he would take the guilt on his own head—if guilt there were. He swore this by his sword and by the Koran. I then commanded that the prisoner be stripped, and that he be bound on the calfskin, and that the mask be torn from his face. These things were done. At last, Yaqub's stricken eyes could see the face—it was his own. He was filled with fear and madness. I gripped his trembling hand in mine, which was steady, and I ordered him to go on witnessing the ceremony of his death. He was possessed by the mirror, so much so that he attempted neither to avert his eyes nor to spill the ink. When in the vision the sword fell on the guilty head, Yaqub moaned with a sound that left my pity untouched, and he tumbled to the floor, dead.

Glory be to Him, who endureth forever, and in whose hand are the keys of unlimited Pardon and unending Punishment.

From *The Lake Regions of Central Equatorial Africa* (1860)
by Richard F. Burton

A Double for Mohammed

A Double for Mohammed

Since the idea of Mohammed is so closely associated with religion in the minds of Muslims, the Lord has ordained that they should be presided over in Heaven by someone impersonating Mohammed. This delegate is not always the same person. A native of Saxony who in earthly life was taken prisoner by the Algerines and became a Muslim once held this position. Having been a Christian, he was moved to speak to them of the Lord, and to say that He was not Joseph's son but the Son of God; it was found advisable to have this man replaced. The office of the representative Mohammed is marked by a torchlike flame, visible only to Muslims.

The real Mohammed, who wrote the Koran, is no longer visible to his followers. I have been informed that at first he presided over them, but that because he strove to rule like God he was deposed and sent away to the south. A certain community of Muslims was once instigated by evil spirits to acknowledge Mohammed as God. To allay the disturbance,

Mohammed was brought up from the nether earth and shown to them, and on this occasion I also saw him. He resembled the bodily spirits who have no interior perception, and his face was very dark. I heard him utter these words: "I am your Mohammed"; and thereupon he sank down again.

From *Vera Christiana Religio* (1771)
by Emanuel Swedenborg

The Generous Enemy

The Generous Enemy

In the year 1102, Magnus Barfod undertook the general conquest of the Irish kingdoms; it is said that on the eve of his death he received this greeting from Muirchertach, the King of Dublin:

May gold and the storm fight on your side, Magnus Barfod.

May your fighting meet with good fortune, tomorrow, on the fields of my kingdom.

May your royal hands strike awe, weaving the sword's web.

May those who oppose your sword be food for the red swan.

May your many gods sate you with glory, may they sate you with blood.

May you be victorious in the dawn, King who tread upon Ireland.

May tomorrow shine the brightest of all your many days.

Because it will be your last. That I swear to you, King Magnus.

Because before its light is blotted out I will defeat you and blot you out, Magnus Barfod.

From the *Anhang zur Heimskringla* (1893) by H. Gering
[Translated by W. S. Merwin]

Of Exactitude in Science

Of Exactitude in Science

. . . In that Empire, the craft of Cartography attained such Perfection that the Map of a Single province covered the space of an entire City, and the Map of the Empire itself an entire Province. In the course of Time, these Extensive maps were found somehow wanting, and so the College of Cartographers evolved a Map of the Empire that was of the same Scale as the Empire and that coincided with it point for point. Less attentive to the Study of Cartography, succeeding Generations came to judge a map of such Magnitude cumbersome, and, not without Irreverence, they abandoned it to the Rigors of sun and Rain. In the western Deserts, tattered Fragments of the Map are still to be found, Sheltering an occasional Beast or beggar; in the whole Nation, no other relic is left of the Discipline of Geography.

From *Travels of Praiseworthy Men* (1658)
by J. A. Suárez Miranda

List of Sources

THE DREAD REDEEMER LAZARUS MORELL
Life on the Mississippi by Mark Twain. New York, 1883.
Mark Twain's America by Bernard De Voto. Boston, 1932.

TOM CASTRO, THE IMPLAUSIBLE IMPOSTOR
The Encyclopædia Britannica (Eleventh Edition). Cambridge, 1911.

THE WIDOW CHING, LADY PIRATE
The History of Piracy by Philip Gosse. London, New York, and Toronto,
   1932.

MONK EASTMAN, PURVEYOR OF INIQUITIES
The Gangs of New York by Herbert Asbury. New York, 1928.

THE DISINTERESTED KILLER BILL HARRIGAN
A Century of Gunmen by Frederick Watson. London, 1931.
The Saga of Billy the Kid by Walter Noble Burns. Garden City, 1926.

THE INSULTING MASTER OF ETIQUETTE KÔTSUKÉ NO SUKÉ
Tales of Old Japan by A. B. Mitford. London, 1871.

THE MASKED DYER, HAKIM OF MERV
A History of Persia by Sir Percy Sykes. London, 1915.
Die Vernichtung der Rose, nach dem arabischen Urtext übertragen von
   Alexander Schulz. Leipzig, 1927.

143

Bibliographical Note

The original titles and first newspaper or magazine appearances of the pieces in this volume are as follows (place of publication, throughout, is Buenos Aires):

THE DREAD REDEEMER LAZARUS MORELL: "El espantoso redentor Lazarus Morell" (entitled "HISTORIA UNIVERSAL DE LA INFAMIA [:] El Espantoso Redentor Lázarus Morell"), *Crítica* (August 12, 1933).

MONK EASTMAN, PURVEYOR OF INIQUITIES: "El proveedor de iniquidades Monk Eastman" (entitled "HISTORIA UNIVERSAL DE LA IN-FAMIA [:] Eastman, el Proveedor de Iniquidades"), *Crítica* (August 19, 1933).

THE WIDOW CHING, LADY PIRATE: "La viuda Ching, pirata" (entitled "Historia Universal de la Infamia [:] La Viuda Ching" and later, when first collected, "La viuda Ching, pirata puntual"), *Crítica* (August 26, 1933).

THE WIZARD POSTPONED: "El brujo postergado" (entitled "El Brujo Postergado" and unsigned), *Crítica* (September 2, 1933).

STREETCORNER MAN: "Hombre de la esquina rosada" (entitled "Hombres de las orillas" and signed "F. Bustos"), *Crítica* (September 16, 1933).

TOM CASTRO, THE IMPLAUSIBLE IMPOSTOR: "El impostor inverosímil Tom Castro" (entitled "Historia Universal de la Infamia [:] El Impostor Invero-símil Tom Castro"), *Crítica* (September 30, 1933).

THE MIRROR OF INK: "El espejo de tinta" (unsigned), *Crítica* (September 30, 1933).

THE CHAMBER OF STATUES: "La cámara de las estatuas" (entitled "La Cámara de las Estatuas [:] (Traducido de un texto árabe del siglo XIII)" and unsigned), *Crítica* (December 2, 1933).

THE INSULTING MASTER OF ETIQUETTE KÔTSUKÉ NO SUKÉ: "El incivil maestro de ceremonias Kotsuké no Suké" (entitled "HISTORIA UNIVERSAL DE LA INFAMIA [:] El Incivil Maestro de Ceremonias Kotsuké no Suké"), *Crítica* (December 9, 1933).

THE MASKED DYER, HAKIM OF MERV: "El tintorero enmascarado Hákim de Merv" (entitled "El Rostro del Profeta"), *Crítica* (January 20, 1934).

A THEOLOGIAN IN DEATH: "Un teólogo en la muerte" (entitled "El Teólogo" and unsigned), *Crítica* (June 23, 1934).

TALE OF THE TWO DREAMERS: "Historia de los dos que soñaron" (entitled "2 Que Soñaron" and unsigned), *Crítica* (June 23, 1934).

OF EXACTITUDE IN SCIENCE: "Del rigor en la ciencia" (attributed, as an excerpt from "VIAJES DE VARONES PRUDENTES, *libro cuarto, cap. XIV, Lérida, 1658,*" to one "Suárez Miranda," the piece was written by Borges with Adolfo Bioy Casares, and was collected by them under the heading "MUSEO"), *Los Anales de Buenos Aires* ([March 1946]).

A DOUBLE FOR MOHAMMED: "Un doble de Mahoma" (collected, under the heading "MUSEO," by "B. Lynch Davis," a pseudonym for Jorge Luis Borges and Adolfo Bioy Casares), *Los Anales de Buenos Aires* (May 1946).

THE GENEROUS ENEMY: "El enemigo generoso" (collected in B. Lynch Davis' MUSEO), *Los Anales de Buenos Aires* (October 1946).

All of the pieces listed above, except for the last three, were first collected in *Historia universal de la infamia* (Tor, 1935); "Del rigor en la ciencia," "Un doble de Mahoma," and "El enemigo generoso" were collected in the book's second edition (Emecé, 1954).

"El asesino desinteresado Bill Harrigan" (THE DISINTERESTED KILLER BILL HARRIGAN) did not appear anywhere before its publication in book form in the first edition.

Historia universal de la infamia was originally published by Editorial Tor as the third volume in the "Colección Megáfono" and printed in July, 1935.